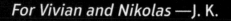

For Vivian and Nikolas —J. K.

For my husband, Scott;
you'll always be my Valenslime! —A. B.

A Feiwel and Friends Book

An imprint of Macmillan Publishing Group, LLC

120 Broadway, New York, NY 10271

mackids.com

Valenslime. Text copyright © 2021 by Joy Keller. Illustrations copyright © 2021 by Ashley Belote.

All rights reserved. Printed in China by RR Donnelley Asia Printing Solutions Ltd., Dongguan City, Guangdong Province.

Our books may be purchased in bulk for promotional, educational, or business use.

Please contact your local bookseller or the Macmillan Corporate and Premium Sales Department

at (800) 221-7945 ext. 5442 or by email at MacmillanSpecialMarkets@macmillan.com.

Library of Congress Cataloging-in-Publication Data is available.

ISBN 978-1-250-79977-7 (hardcover)

Book design by Cindy De la Cruz

Feiwel and Friends logo designed by Filomena Tuosto

First edition, 2021

1 3 5 7 9 10 8 6 4 2

VALENSLIME

Written by **Joy Keller**

Illustrated by **Ashley Belote**

Feiwel and Friends

New York

Victoria Franken was a
slime scientist.
She loved her slime.

Her slime, Goop,
loved her back.

He bubbled with enthusiasm when they experimented in the lab.

He oozed contentment when they read science books together.

He bounced along happily when they walked Igor in the park.

Yes, ever since the stormy night Victoria brought Goop to life, the two had enjoyed their time together.

When Valentine's Day rolled around, Victoria made twenty slime cards for her school friends, a doggy-bone card for Igor, and one extra-special card for the slime. As she admired her cutting and gluing, Victoria realized something.

She had LOTS of friends. Goop only had one friend. Her. That didn't seem fair.

Luckily, Victoria had an idea.
"Igor! We must experiment!"

Victoria and Igor gathered
materials, snuck to the attic,
and locked the door behind them.
If Goop couldn't make a new friend,
Victoria would make a new friend for him!

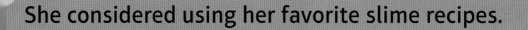
She considered using her favorite slime recipes.

Snifftastic
Flower Slime.

Mouthwatering
Chocolate Slime.

Magical Fairy Slime.

But none of these slimes seemed quite right.

Now all she had to do was wait for a lightning storm
and—*ZAP!*—her creation would jolt to life!

She waited.

And waited.

And waited.

Victoria sighed.
It looked like
lightning wouldn't
strike. She would
have to take matters
into her own hands.

Lightning
Slime

"Igor—
fetch me
some wires!"

After tinkering and tuning,
Victoria was finally ready.
She hit the switch.

The slime foamed and frothed.
It splattered and sparkled.
It sent a cloud of sugar into the air.

Victoria held her breath as the glittery, gooey creature crept over the side of the beaker. This was it! She had done it! She had made a friend for—

UH-OH.

The slime was still growing. Bigger . . . and bigger . . . and bigger. Before long, it stretched all the way to the ceiling.

Victoria had to do
something. Fast.
"Igor! Pull the plug!"

But the slime kept growing.

She tried to catch it. "Igor! The vacuum!"

But the slime wouldn't be contained.

She attempted to freeze it.
"Igor! Ice cubes!"

But the slime wouldn't stop.
Victoria and Igor slipped from the room
as the shimmery goop filled the attic.

Just as it started to squeeze
out the door after them—

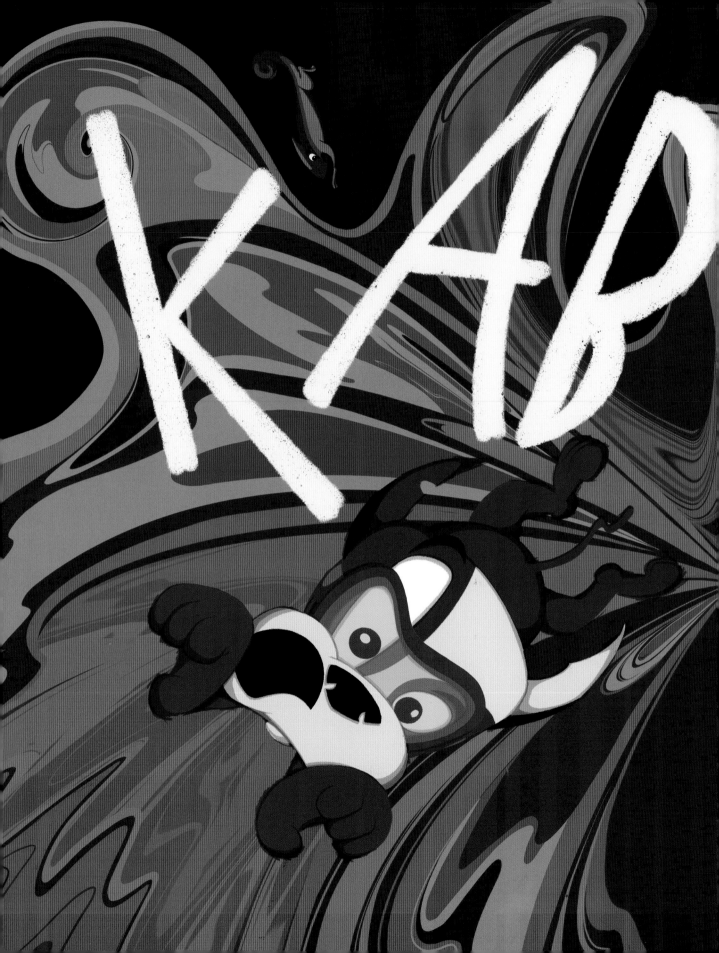

The giant slime burst into ten regular-sized slimes.

Victoria and Igor
stared in shock.
What had she done?
She hadn't made
Goop a new friend . . .

. . . she'd made
him LOTS of
new friends!

Victoria introduced Goop to her latest creations.
The slime quivered with happiness.
From that day forward, Goop and the other
slimes spent a lot of time together.

They did their own experiments.

They played slime games.

They taught Igor new tricks.

Goop was thrilled with his new friends . . .

But that didn't change the fact that
Victoria would always be his *best* friend.
He loved her.
And Victoria loved him back.

From the Lab of Victoria Franken

Snifftastic Flower Slime

Materials
½ cup flower-scented hair conditioner
food coloring (optional)
1 cup corn starch

Try making your own valenslimes! Here are some of Victoria's favorite festive slime recipes (guaranteed NOT to come to life).

For each recipe, you'll need a medium mixing bowl, measuring cups, measuring spoons, and a mixing spoon.

Steps

1. Put the conditioner in a bowl.

2. The slime will be the color of the conditioner. If you don't like that color, add a few drops of food coloring to change it.

3. Add ¼ cup of the cornstarch at a time, until the slime starts to form.

4. Work the mixture in your hands until it's the right consistency.

5. Play with your super-smelling flower slime!

Be sure to ask an adult to be your lab assistant!

Try different conditioners to find the scent you like best. If you don't like flowers, you can use a fruity-scented conditioner, instead!

BE MINE

Mouthwatering Chocolate Slime

Materials
1 bag large marshmallows
microwave-safe bowl
2 tablespoons cocoa powder
1 cup powdered sugar
cutting board or cookie sheet

You should never taste a science experiment—except this one! Victoria's favorite dessert is this delicious and completely edible chocolate slime.

Steps

1. Put the marshmallows in the microwave-safe bowl. Have an adult microwave the marshmallows for 20 seconds, then stir them. Microwave them for another 20 seconds and stir again. If your marshmallows haven't melted, microwave at 10-second intervals until they do. Be careful not to burn them!

2. Mix in cocoa powder.

3. Mix in ½ cup of the powdered sugar. The slime will be very sticky at this point, so it may be hard to stir.

4. Get a cutting board or cookie sheet to be your work surface, and dust it with powdered sugar. Dust your hands with powdered sugar, too! Place the slime on your work surface and knead in as much sugar as you can. This will decrease the stickiness and make it fun to stretch.

Edible slime doesn't have the same consistency as play slime. If it's too soft for you, try substituting ¼ cup cornstarch for ¼ cup of the powdered sugar to firm up your chocolate slime. (Just understand that it won't taste quite as good.)

5. Play with your chocolate slime! When it starts to get too sticky (it *is* marshmallow, after all), add some more powdered sugar. And when you're done playing, have a snack!

I ♡ chocolate

Magical Fairy Slime

Materials

¼ cup warm water
½ teaspoon baking soda
¾ cup clear school glue (or 6 oz)
glitter
food coloring (optional)
1 tablespoon saline solution

Fairies like anything that glitters, so try adding sequins or small beads for an extra-magical effect!

Steps

1. Mix the warm water and baking soda in a bowl until the baking soda dissolves.

2. Add the glue. Mix gently to avoid bubbles.

3. Mix in as much glitter as you'd like! (Victoria likes to use pink glitter, but you can use any color.) You can also add a few drops of food coloring for brighter slime.

4. Slowly add the saline solution, stirring as you go.

5. Work the slime in your hands. Rub a little saline solution on your hands first to prevent the slime from sticking to your fingers. Keep going until it's the right consistency. (If it's too sticky, try adding some more saline solution. If it's too rubbery or breaks easily, add a little lotion or warm water.)

6. Play with your sparkly fairy slime!

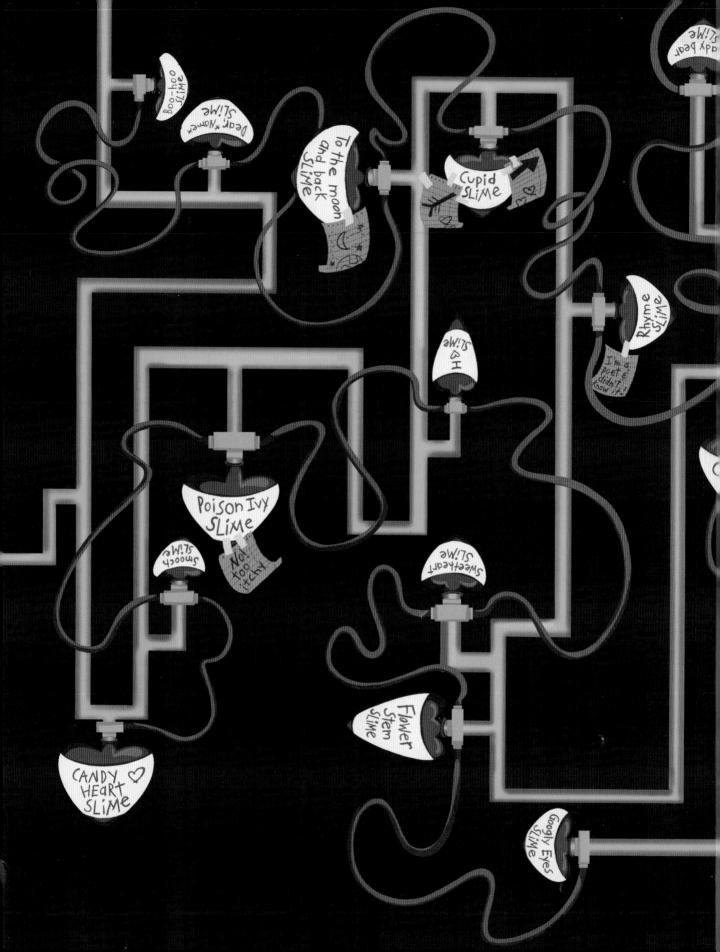

feng shui garden design
Creating Serenity

風水 feng shui garden design
Creating Serenity

by Antonia Beattie
Photography by Leigh Clapp
Consultant: Bill Wilson

PERIPLUS

First published in North America and Asia in 2003
by Periplus Editions (HK) Ltd.

© Copyright 2003 Lansdowne Publishing Pty Ltd

Library of Congress Cataloging-in-Publication Data is available.
ISBN 0-7946-5016-3

DISTRIBUTED BY

North America, Latin America,
(English language)
Tuttle Publishing
364 Innovation Drive
North Clarendon
VT 05759-9436
Tel: (802) 773-8930
Tel: (800) 526-2778
info@tuttlepublishing.com

Japan and Korea
Tuttle Publishing
Yaekari Bldg., 3rd Floor
5-4-12 Osaki Shinagawa-ku
Tokyo 141-0032
Tel: (81) 35-437-0171
Fax: (81) 35-437-0755
tuttle–sales@gol.com

Asia Pacific
Berkeley Books Pte. Ltd.
130 Joo Seng Road
#06-01/03
Singapore 368357
Tel: (65) 6280-3320
Fax: (65) 6280-6290
inquiries@periplus.com.sg

Commissioned by Deborah Nixon
Text: Antonia Beattie
Photography: Leigh Clapp
Feng Shui Consultant: Bill Wilson
Illustration: Jane Cameron
Design: Robyn Latimer
Copy Editor: Sarah Shrubb
Production Manager: Sally Stokes
Project Coordinator: Kate Merrifield

First Edition
06 05 04 03   10 9 8 7 6 5 4 3 2 1

Set in Gill Sans, Officina Sans, Ruling Script,
Trebuchet and Present on QuarkXPress
Printed in Singapore

Contents

Introduction:
The Garden as a Sanctuary for the Soul 8

The Basics of Feng Shui 10
• How Feng Shui works
• The art of placement in the garden: observing nature
• Balance and harmony: the flow of yin and yang
• Garden design and good Feng Shui

The Chinese System of the Elements 18
• How the five elements work in the garden
• Earth • Metal • Water • Wood • Fire
• Balancing your garden design

Applying Feng Shui Principles to
Garden Design 26
• Some important Feng Shui tools
• Using the bagua with your garden plan
• Analyzing your site: symmetry and shape
• The effect of your surroundings

The Eight Aspirations 34
• What are the eight aspirations in Feng Shui?
• Improving prosperity
• Getting the acknowledgment you deserve
• Improving your love life
• Enhancing creativity
• Finding helpful people
•Strengthening your career path
• Helping your studies
• Improving your health

Attracting Qi 46

• Harmonizing with nature • The entrance
• Paths and pavements • Plants to attract
beneficial energy • Trees, hedges and screens
• Water features • Garden statues • Garden ornaments
• Outdoor furniture • Garden structures
• Garden lighting

Small-Scale Feng Shui Gardens 68

• Feng Shui in small spaces: intimate designs
• Small-scale gardens: beauty and harmony
in miniature • Courtyards • Terraces
• Balconies • Window boxes

Feng Shui Cures 76

• Solving energy flow problems
• Deflecting poison arrows
• Light • Color • Sound • Water
• Solid Objects • Movement

Seasonal Qi: Putting It All Together 94

• Tapping into seasonal energy for a lush, healthy
garden • The seasons and the five elements
• Winter • Spring • Summer • High summer • Autumn

Plant List 103

Glossary 108

Acknowledgments 109

Index 110

Introduction

The Garden as a Sanctuary for the Soul

Opposite: The principles of Feng Shui can be applied with startling results to almost any garden to improve the flow of energy. You will eventually see a vast improvement in the way your garden looks and feels, enticing you to spend more time outside.

Below: Feng shui principles, such as incorporating more curves in your furniture design and the placement and installation of a fountain, will help you create restful areas in your home and garden where you can feel totally relaxed.

The garden has for centuries been used as a place of meditation, relaxation and contemplation. In these hectic, stressful times, the garden is as important as ever. A peaceful, healthy garden space, whether it is a sizable garden surrounding your home or a couple of potted plants on a windy balcony, can be re-created to provide a sanctuary for the soul. One way of creating such a garden is by using the ancient Chinese techniques of Feng Shui.

Feng Shui is a centuries-old method of shaping a beneficial, intangible life force. This life force, called chi or qi, is believed to permeate all things and is created by the continuous balance of complementary forces called yin and yang. The reason for manipulating this energy is to achieve a harmonious environment around us. Feng Shui practitioners believe that once this energy is allowed to flow around our garden and home in a gentle way, it will also clear the blockages and obstacles that we experience in life.

Many people in many civilizations believe everything in the world is closely interconnected. If we change our environment, we change our lives. By clearing our house and developing our garden along Feng Shui lines, we can find harmony, peace and success.

The garden has often been a neglected area, as many of us find we have less and less time to maintain and tend a garden. However, if you set aside just a little bit of time in the week for this most pleasurable task, you can make some startling changes in the space around your home. By implementing even the most basic Feng Shui gardening principles, you will improve the flow of beneficial and protective energy to your home.

By tapping into the power of Feng Shui and its ancient wisdom you will not only experience the benefits that the flow of nurturing energy can bring, but you will be able to link into the rhythms and cycles of nature, and that will inspire you to incorporate more of nature's balance and harmony into your life.

How Feng Shui works

There are some concepts we need to understand if we are to use Feng Shui effectively. First, according to Feng Shui beliefs, energy – or qi – flows through the world in either a beneficial or an unsettling manner, according to the shape of the environment and the placement of certain objects. There is a powerful link between the flow of beneficial energy through your garden and home and the success and luck that you experience in your life. Second, the circulation of this energy is powered by the constant interaction of two opposing forces, called yin (passive or negative energy) and yang (active or positive energy) (pages 14–15). Third, in Chinese philosophy, everything in the universe is made up of a blend of five elements. These elements are Earth, Metal, Water, Wood and Fire.

There are also a number of schools of Feng Shui belief, including the form or landscape school of Feng Shui, which deals with the location and energies of the four Celestial animals. Where these creatures are situated in your property can influence the type of energy that flows from the four cardinal points of the compass.

There is a Feng Shui template for the most beneficial placement of your entire home and garden – one example of the ideal would be a spot halfway up a mountain, where the flow of cosmic and earth-created energies is balanced by having the mountains at your back and a gently curving river and an undulating hill in front of you. However, as most of us do not have homes and gardens in a place like this, Feng Shui practitioners have developed a great number of methods or "cures" (pages 76–93) to help us attract beneficial energy or block the flow of harmful energy to our homes and gardens, no matter where they are.

By adding certain symbolic objects to your home or garden – elements that represent missing aspects of the Feng Shui template (pages 12–13) or that rebalance the elements or the forces of yin and yang in your space – you can create a sanctuary of positive energy.

Opposite: Garden ornaments, plants, rocks, paths, differently shaped shrubs and variously colored flowers all correspond with a particular Chinese element – either earth, metal, water, wood or fire. A garden in which all the five elements are represented and placed in balance with each other will generate beneficial energy in your environment and life.

The art of placement in the garden: observing nature

Above: Someone sitting in the middle of this beautiful garden will feel comfortable and relaxed, particularly if they sit with the hedge and trees behind them and the sloping flower beds before them. The most auspicious placement of your house or garden arbor is one that is reminiscent of sitting in a comfortable armchair with support for your back, comfortable armrests on either side and a footstool in front.

Through the meticulous observation of nature, Feng Shui practitioners developed a template for the perfect placement of a house and its surrounding environment, a situation that encourages the flow of beneficial energy, which in turn improves the eight aspirations of wealth, fame, relationships, creativity, mentorship, career, knowledge and health (pages 34–45), and improves the growth and health of plants in the garden.

The most auspicious position for a house and garden is, as mentioned earlier, midway up a mountain (representing a balance between the energies of the cosmos and earth), facing a gently curving river and a small undulating hill and backed by the mountain, very much like a person reclining comfortably in an armchair with a footstool at their feet.

The gently curving river and undulating hill symbolize the flow of beneficial, lucky energy, which is represented as the Celestial Red Phoenix. This energy represents a southerly energy full of good fortune, as well as the energy of summer, and flows best when you have a pleasant view or sense of openness visible from your front yard.

The mountains, like the backrest of a comfortable armchair, symbolize support; this supportive energy is represented in Feng Shui as the Celestial Black Tortoise. This energy represents a northerly, nurturing energy, as well as the energy of winter.

Feng Shui garden tip

If the Tiger (west) side of your property is higher or larger than the Dragon (east) side, consider installing garden lighting in the west part of your garden to keep the Tiger energy subdued.

On the sides of the property, the Celestial White Tiger symbolizes the west, and the Celestial Green Dragon symbolizes the east. The energy of the west represents a time of harvest, like autumn, while the arousing of yang energy takes place in the east, like spring.

As qi flows beneficially along curved lines, the house and garden are best positioned in an environment of undulating hills and gently winding rivers. This can be symbolically echoed in a garden by creating curving paths (pages 50–51), rounded garden beds, and raised and lowered areas of garden space. Water is also an essential feature of a garden – it is believed that every garden should, if possible, feature a pond or fountain, with a pump so that the water is in constant, gentle motion and does not grow stagnant (pages 56–57).

Where energy is not allowed to move or is blocked, it will become stagnant and will attract clutter, overgrowth or dry patches in the garden. Symbols of stagnant energy, such as dead trees, are best removed, as they create a stab of negative energy, called a poison arrow (or sha qi), that can hit the house or another part of the garden causing energy flow problems.

Other objects that create poison arrows in the environment around you include telephone poles and flagpoles; straight, sharply angled rooflines; and the corners of house or garden structures. Qi becomes harmful when it is allowed to flow along straight lines, so roads aimed directly at your property will also create poison arrows — this will cause a speeding up of energy that will affect the wellbeing of those living in your home.

Placing hedges, shrubs or ponds between these objects and your house or garden will help screen you from their negative energies (pages 52–55). These objects and plants are listed among the Feng Shui cures used to correct the flow of energy in your house and garden (pages 76–93).

The presence and balance of the landscape formation of the four celestial animals are crucial. These animals are not always assigned to a particular compass direction. According to form school Feng Shui (also known as landscape Feng Shui), their locations are determined by the direction a building faces. Standing with your back to the front of the building and looking in the direction the building faces, the tortoise is behind the building, the phoenix is in front, the dragon is on your left and the tiger is on your right.

Above: Ponds and fountains are very important features of any garden design that follow Feng Shui principles. However, it is important that the yin quality of water is balanced by a yang feature, such as (in this case) the red colored, square columns forming the covered walkway surrounding the pool.

Balance and harmony: the flow of yin and yang

In Feng Shui, to create a beneficial flow of energy in the garden there must be a balance between yang and yin elements. Yang energy is seen in a form of active masculine energy that also corresponds to the sun and bright colors, such as reds, oranges and yellows, while yin energy is passive feminine energy that also corresponds to the moon and cool colors, such as blues and greens. The front yard, a public area, represents yang energy; the back yard, a more private area, represents yin energy.

If there is too much yang energy (for instance, if the garden is very sunny with lots of colorful plants and ornaments), the area will feel very active. If there is too much yin energy (for instance, if the garden is constantly in the shade and there is a pond that is still), the area will feel passive.

Draw a small map of your main garden area, then walk around it and shade those areas that you believe correspond with yin energy – areas that are wet, soft, shaded, recessed or level, such as a recessed play area or the lawn. Leave clear all areas that are yang – dry, hard, sunny areas or areas that are elevated, such as raised garden beds.

Do the same for the other substantial sections of your garden: the front garden, between the street and your front door, and, if the areas are large enough, either side of the house.

These maps will be your starting point when you begin to rearrange your garden according to good Feng Shui design. If you have noticed that you have too much of yang energy in the garden, clear the clutter, weed the garden beds, plant dark-leafed shrubs or install a pond or water feature. If the energy is too yin, consider installing appropriate garden lighting in the area, removing the pond or moving a structure that is casting too much shadow in the area.

Above: In the garden, yang energy is generated by garden structures such as decking, pergolas, garden sheds and other small buildings and is also found in the sunny areas of the garden.

Opposite: A balance of light and dark areas in the garden help generate the flow of beneficial energy. Yin energy is found in shady areas and in the space between structures, trees and other features. Views of gentle hills with a stream or creek at the base, or of serene woods or forests, are believed to provide a flow of lucky energy.

Garden design and good Feng Shui

Good Feng Shui occurs when energy is allowed to flow harmoniously within your immediate environment. Focus first on the front garden, as it is the first area to receive the flow of beneficial energy from the environment. The energy flows into your front garden through the main entrance, called the "mouth of qi."

It is imperative that energy is allowed to meander in this part of the garden. Avoid straight paths or driveways. If you already have straight paths, consider replacing them or planting shrubs or ground cover which will encroach onto the flat surface of the path(s) and hide the straight lines. If you decide to plant shrubs, remember to choose plants that have a shallow root system so that the roots do not eventually raise or crack the path or driveway.

The back yard represents support and nurture. If this area feels too open or slopes away from the house, plant hedges or trees that will grow tall and strong along the back boundary line of the yard. These trees or tall shrubs will symbolize the supportive energy of the mountains that should ideally be situated at the back of your property (see the Feng Shui template, for the most auspicious positioning of a home and garden, on pages 12–13).

Use a compass to find out which direction your front yard faces. Each direction attracts a certain kind of energy (pages 12–13). Ideally, your front yard should face south, which attracts a yang or lucky form of energy. If your front yard does not face south, but you wish to attract this energy into your garden, place a statue or image of a Red Phoenix in the garden.

If your front yard faces west, keep the area as still and quiet as possible; any planting should be low-growing. A north-facing garden attracts energy supportive of your career; this can be enhanced by incorporating a pond or other water feature within view of the front door. An east-facing garden invites energy supportive of family relations; this energy can be enhanced by introducing specimen plants, in particular, bamboo.

Above and opposite: Beneficial energy meanders. To encourage this energy to move around your garden, install curved pathways and garden beds. Let plants grow over any straight edgings to slow down the flow of energy, which would normally shoot down a straight path.

Feng Shui garden tip

Have only healthy, vibrant plants in your garden, preferably plants with variegated foliage or that produce an abundance of flowers.

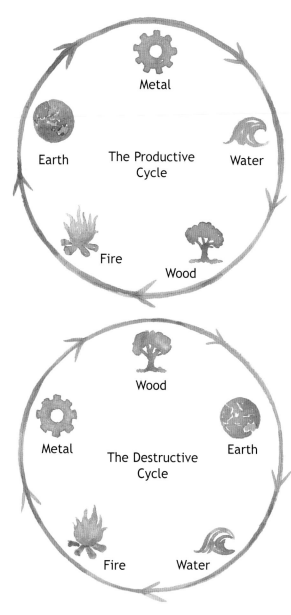

Above: Use these flowcharts to understand the interrelationship between the elements. Follow the direction of the arrows on each circle to see how one element supports the other (for example, Wood fuels Fire) or how one element can destroy another (for example, Water extinguishes Fire).

How the five elements work in the garden

In keeping with the theory of the interconnectedness of everything, the five Chinese elements – Earth, Metal, Wood, Fire and Water – correspond with certain numbers, compass directions, life aspirations, life paths, seasons and other aspects of life. Certain common objects can symbolize or represent the elements, such as earthenware pots for earth, metal gardening tools for metal, timber garden furniture for wood, the barbecue for fire and a pond for water.

In Chinese medicine, the human body is believed to be made up of a combination or balance of the elements, so ill health can be rectified by removing certain foods or by adding medicine that resonates with a particular element or combination of elements. Similarly, in Feng Shui, the elements can be used to rectify an imbalance in the flow of energy around a garden or home.

These five elements are believed to interact with each other in both productive and destructive ways. In the productive cycle (see illustration above left), the Earth produces Metal, Metal contains Water, Water replenishes Wood, Wood helps fuel a Fire, and Fire aids the Earth. In the destructive cycle (see illustration bottom left), Earth muddies Water, Water quenches Fire, Fire melts Metal, Metal chops Wood, and Wood depletes the Earth.

Objects and combinations of plantings that reflect the destructive cycle of the elements will attract negative energy in the form of accidents, feelings of unrest, and poor growth. For instance, do not have a pond or water feature right next to the barbecue, as Water is a destructive element to Fire. Remove either one of these features or install an object that corresponds to Wood, such as a wooden decking, so that the destructive relationship between the pond and barbecue is broken (see page 25 for other creative solutions).

Harmonious combinations of the elements in garden ornament and plantings include red roses planted next to a wooden fence (Wood and Fire), a paved barbecue area (Fire and Earth), terracotta pots beside a metal gate (Earth and Metal), a metal birdbath filled with water (Metal and Water) and a dense planting of hedges around a pond (Water and Wood). By thinking in terms of the five elements, you will quickly be able to assess why a particular area feels harmonious or disruptive in energy.

Below: Here is an example of a supportive relationship between the elements of metal, represented by the metal crane scupltures, and water. There is also harmony between yin and yang energies as a sprinkling of pink (yang) colored flowers balance the dark foliage around the waterfall.

Earth

The element of Earth corresponds with the energy of high summer in the Chinese system of seasons (page 100). This is the time when yin and yang energies are in balance. This element also corresponds with an area that is central in a garden or home, or with the compass directions of southwest and northwest.

Garden objects that are symbolic of the Earth element include rock gardens, large terracotta pots, brick or stone walls and clay paving stones forming a path through the garden. Sheds with flat roofs or square shapes are also symbolic of the Earth element.

Plants that correspond to the energy of the Earth element include sweet-smelling herbs, such as rosemary and sage, and flowers that are yellow or orange, such as deep yellow chrysanthemums, marigolds, wallflowers, nasturtiums, and primroses. In Feng Shui, chrysanthemums are believed to evoke a happy and joyful energy in the garden.

In your rock garden, include plants such as yellow rock rose and evening primrose. You can also include roses in terracotta pots. Yew can also be planted, as well as other trees or shrubs that are shaped like a square (pages 52–53).

Objects and plants corresponding with the element of Earth must not be placed near objects and plants corresponding with Water (page 22), but will benefit the element of Metal (page 21). Also keep Earth away from the element of Wood (page 23), as Wood has a hindering effect on Earth, although the energy of the earth is obviously necessary for the growth of wood.

Above and left: Rich yellow flowers, rocks, pebbles and gravel are all symbolic of the happy, stable energy of the Earth elements.

Metal

The element of Metal corresponds with the energy of autumn in the Chinese system of seasons (page 101). This is the time when yin energy is beginning to dominate, as the energy of the earth begins to burrow into the ground. This element also corresponds with a westerly direction.

Garden objects that are symbolic of the Metal element include bronze and other metal sculptures, large metal containers, metal dome-shaped structures or spheres, sundials, metal furniture, posts and frames, as well as tin panels and roofs.

Plants that correspond to the energy of the Metal element include herbs such as yarrow and wormwood. Catmint is also a Metal element herb – plant it along paths to soften both the color of the garden and the edges of the path. White flowers such as chrysanthemums, honesty, roses, gardenias, arum lily (or calla) and snowdrops also symbolize Metal.

Plants with gray–green leaves, such as lamb's ears and artemisia, plants with variegated leaves, such as Coprosma "Variegata," and trees or shrubs that have a circular shape (pages 52–53) are also characteristic of the Metal element.

Objects and plants that correspond to the element of Metal must not be placed near objects and plants that correspond to Wood (page 23), but they will benefit the element of Water (page 22).

Above: Metal pots, buckets and recycled metal objects, such as old metal wheelbarrows filled with flowers or other plants evoke the Metal element in a garden.

Right: A metal gate like this one is not only symbolic of Metal but its open, curved design allows the beneficial energy to flow through into a new area of the garden with little hinderance.

Water

The element of Water corresponds to the energy of winter in the Chinese system of seasons (page 97). This is the time when yin energy is at its strongest, as most of the earth's energy is deeply underground. This element also corresponds to a northerly compass direction.

Garden objects that are symbolic of the Water element include water features such as ponds, fountains and waterfalls. Swimming pools, as well as bathhouses sheltering a spa, are also symbolic of the element of Water.

Plants that correspond to the energy of Water include plants that are blue or tending towards black, such as some violets. Other Water flowers include cyclamen and violas. Herbs such as mint, thyme and chives are considered Water plants.

Trees that are symbolic of the element of Water include magnolia, silver birch, dogwood, juniper, honeysuckle and tea tree.

When installing a pond, always make sure to keep a water pump operational at all times and in good condition so that the pond will not become stagnant or overgrown. Around the edges of the pool, plant white flowers or gray-green plants in an undulating line (a "shape" or silhouette that corresponds to the Water element; pages 52–53).

Objects and plants that relate to the element of Water will benefit Wood (page 23), and Metal (page 21) will benefit Water objects and plants. Keep Water away from the element of Earth (page 20), as it has a hindering effect on Water.

Below: A large water feature attracts a lot of yin energy – it is fine in a public garden or a large-sized residential property. However, always remember to install a water feature that is in proportion to the rest of your garden – do not allow it to dominate your garden space.

Wood

The element of Wood corresponds to the energy of spring in the Chinese system of seasons (page 98). This is the time when yang energy is becoming dominant. This element also corresponds to an easterly compass direction.

Garden objects that symbolize the Wood element include wooden furniture, wooden structures such as decking, lattice fences, wooden fences, posts and pergolas, wicker furniture, and wooden stakes and garden bed edgings.

Plants that correspond to the energy of the Wood element include evergreens such as conifers and English boxwood. These trees are dense and green, and are excellent for the edging of a garden or for screening hedges. Camellias, hydrangeas and pitto-sporums, as well as other plants considered rectangular in shape (pages 52–53), are also symbolic of the element of Wood and are excellent plantings for screening in the garden.

Hostas, woodruffs, and primulas, as well as such herbs as basil and parsley, also symbolize Wood.

Characteristics of Wood plants include deep, lush green leaves and, usually, dense growth. Plants that do not represent Wood include those that have thorns (for example, some roses), needles, pointed leaves, or that are miniature in nature.

Water (page 22) will benefit Wood objects and plants, and Wood benefits Fire (page 24). Keep the element of Metal (page 21) away from Wood.

Below: Wooden playhouses attract the spring-like energy of young children at play. To minimize accidents, add more yin energy to the site, such as planting shrubs with dark foliage around the playhouse or painting one feature of the playhouse in yin colours, such as blues or greens.

Fire

The element of Fire corresponds to the energy of summer in the Chinese system of seasons (page 99). This is the time when yang energies are at their height. This element also corresponds to a southerly compass direction.

Garden objects that are symbolic of the Fire element include barbecues and other cooking apparatus in the garden, such as open ovens, and pointed structures used in stacking trailing plants, particularly red tomatoes.

Plants that correspond to the energy of the Fire element include those that produce red flowers or leaves and those with sharp leaf shapes or spiky thorns. Triangle-shaped plants also resonate with the element of Fire (pages 52–53). Fire plants include pine trees, firs, cypresses, bird of paradise shrubs, and crimson-leafed plum trees. In Feng Shui, the pine tree is symbolic of longevity.

Fire flowers include red roses, lupins, dahlias, bromeliads, tulips, daffodils, irises, snapdragons and gladioli. Herbs that evoke the Fire element energy include chilies, leeks, garlic, dill and asparagus.

It is important to be sparing with Fire plants, though, as the strength of their energy, through color or through scent, may overwhelm surrounding plants. These plants always look their best when planted against a background of rich, deep green foliage.

Objects and plants that correspond to the element of Fire must not be placed near objects and plants that correspond to Metal (page 21), but will benefit Earth (page 20). Wood (page 23) will benefit Fire objects and plants.

Above: The red of geraniums or maples when their leaves turn in autumn evoke the sparky energy of the Fire element in the garden. The Fire element is strong and can overwhelm surrounding plants, so it is important to use this element sparingly – more as an accent rather than a feature.

Balancing your garden design

Try the following re-harmonizing solutions:

Metal and Wood If you have a destructive arrangement of Metal and Wood (such as a metal shed and dense greenery), add a Water feature or plant to re-harmonize the energy. For instance, do not combine a wooden picket fence with metal posts or place a wooden seat under a weeping willow.

Wood and Earth If you have Wood and Earth arranged together, add a Fire object or a plant nearby to harmonize the energy. Plant some red flowers in a terracotta pot sitting on a wooden deck.

Earth and Water Earth and Water objects and plants must be kept away from each other. They can be re-harmonized by adding Metal objects and plants near them. A terracotta pot filled with water can be a water feature if it has a metal spout or water pump circulating the water.

Water and Fire Use a Wood object or plant to re-harmonize the energy in a Water and Fire area. For instance, install a wooden lattice fence between a water feature and the barbecue area.

Fire and Metal To restore harmony, place an earthenware pot, lay a paved path or use any other Earth object or plant near a Fire and Metal area, such as the barbecue area with a tin shed nearby, or a bed of yellow flowers or a weeping fruit tree.

Top: Use a metal sculpture to balance the tension between stone pavers and a water feature.

Above: White flowers counter the destructive energy generated between a feature symbolic of earth and one representing water.

Some important Feng Shui tools

Above: A pretty, striking garden feature will attract beneficial energy to it and will enhance the corresponding aspiration. Make sure that there is plenty of space around the feature so that the energy can flow unhindered toward it.

Two of the most important Feng Shui garden tools are your compass and the yang bagua (sometimes referred to as the pa kua). Your compass will help you determine which way your garden is facing. Generally, your garden faces the most common entrance into the area. This is the entrance through which energy or qi enters the area.

The front yard generally faces the front boundary line. The back yard may be harder to assess when there are two or more entrances. However, as qi enters the property from the street along the front boundary line, the back yard will be facing the same direction as the front yard. This is so even if the back yard also contains a garage door opening at the back boundary line.

To determine which direction your garden faces, stand at the entrance of qi into the area with your compass, facing away from your garden, and note where the compass needle is pointing.

Compass reading (degrees)	Facing direction
22.5–67.5	Northeast
67.5–112.5	East
112.5–157.5	Southeast
157.5–202.5	South
202.5–247.5	Southwest
247.5–292.5	West
292.2–337.5	Northwest
337.5–22.5	North

Once you know which direction your garden faces, you can then use the yang bagua or pa kua to figure out where the eight aspirations of life fall within your garden. The bagua is an octagonal object where each side represents a compass direction and its corresponding aspiration, such as wealth, fame, relationships, creativity, mentors, career, knowledge and health (pages 34–45). This information is represented by trigrams, a series of three broken or unbroken lines around the edge of the bagua.

As mentioned before, in Feng Shui everything is related and interconnected. The bagua has a central image of the yin and yang symbols, which together form the modern Tai Chi symbol.

Once you know which area corresponds with which aspiration, you can then use simple garden ornaments, objects and plants to increase your success in the aspiration areas of your choice.

Above left: Use sculptures of happy ducks (who are believed to symbolize fidelity and longevity in marriage) in your relationship area or a happy family grouping in your children and creativity sector.

Above center: Use red flowers, such as tulips, in the fame and acknowledgment aspiration to make sure that you are not overlooked for a promotion or an important business contract.

Above right: Use a water feature in your wealth sector, making sure that the water is always kept in motion and that it stays clean and fresh. Flowing water symbolizes the easy passage of money into the family.

Feng Shui garden tip

The yin bagua, or Early Heaven Arrangement, represents the ideal universe and is used as a protective symbol. The yang bagua, or Later Heaven Arrangement, represents the movement and cycles of the earth's natural flow. It is used in a practical way to apply the trigrams to yang areas, such as houses and their gardens.

Using the bagua with your garden plan

The bagua, which is the octagonal disc discussed on page 26, contains brief information about the structure of the world and its energies. Each of the eight sides of the bagua corresponds to, among other things, a particular compass direction and one of the eight aspirations (pages 34–45). At the center of the bagua is a symbol of yin and yang.

There are many schools of thought on how to apply the bagua to a particular area to find out about its energy flow. In this book, we shall focus on finding the center of the area you wish to assess in terms of energy flow, and use a simplified version of the bagua, in the form of a circle subdivided into eight equal segments.

To make your own bagua template, take a piece of tracing paper (letter size or A4) and draw a circle large enough to span the sheet. Find the middle and subdivide the circle into eight equal segments. Label the segments with the names of the eight compass directions most commonly used in Feng Shui – north, northeast, east, southeast, south, southwest, west, and northwest.

Left: The bagua symbolizes the interconnection between the energy of Nature and the many important aspects of our lives. Each compass direction corresponds with one of the eight aspirations. Each aspiration in turn corresponds with the elements, the energies of yin and yang, the dynamics of a family and other connections.

One of the first questions you need to answer before you apply the bagua to your garden or property plan is whether you are focusing on your garden and home as a whole or whether you wish to analyze your front yard and back yard separately.

Many Western properties do not have the luxury of a lot of space along the sides of the house. If your property has a front yard and back yard separated by the house and connected, if at all, by only a narrow pathway on one or both sides of the house, consider treating your front yard and back yard as separate gardens.

If you are treating your front yard and back yard as separate spaces, take a compass reading and work out which direction your garden faces (page 26), then draw a rough sketch of the yard. Whether the garden is symmetrical or not, draw either a square or rectangle around your yard plan. Do not worry that there may be missing or slightly projecting areas within this outline shape.

Find the center of the yard. This can be done easily by drawing diagonal lines connecting the four corners of the outline shape. The middle of your yard is where the diagonal lines meet.

Place the center of your template bagua over the point that represents the middle of your yard, then rotate the template so that the segment of the bagua that corresponds to the relevant compass direction is directly aligned with the front boundary line.

If you would like to treat your house and garden as one unit, find the center of your home by first drawing your property and within it sketching out a rough floor plan of your home. Next, draw a simplified square or rectangular outline around the floor plan and then find the middle of the house by drawing a cross running through the four corners of the outline shape.

Over this point in the house, position the bagua template so that the center of the house and the bagua are matched up and the template reflects the compass direction of the front boundary line. Extend the lines, if necessary, so that the entire property (home and garden) is subdivided into eight segments.

Turn to pages 34–45 to determine the areas of your property that reflect each of the eight Feng Shui aspirations.

Above: The bagua comes in many configurations — with yin and yang symbols, mirrors, red and gold tassles and a decorative red knot — all designed to attract positive, lucky energy and balance into our lives.

Above: Feng Shui is heavily reliant upon you knowing which way your house and garden is facing. Purchase a good quality, reliable compass to help you figure out your directions.

Analyzing your site: symmetry and shape

Balance and symmetry are integral aspects of Feng Shui gardening. The yin and yang symbol, with its two fluid shapes, one black with a dot of white and the other white with a dot of black, blended together to form a circle, is symbolic of the correct flow of energy in an environment. As the front yard tends towards yang energy, always include an object or plant that represents yin energy, such as a pond or a rounded water feature. Similarly, include an object or plant that represents yang energy, such as a small bed of fragrant red flowers or a crimson-leaved tree, in the back yard.

In keeping with this concept of balance, symmetry of shape allows the optimal flow of energy within a property. Squares evoke the energy of the element of Earth (page 20), which is the most stable of energies. Rectangles are symbolic of the energy of Wood (page 23), an energy believed to imbue the residents with a sense of growth and achievement, as well as flexibility and resilience.

Where the area is irregular (L-shaped, for instance) or where the boundary lines meet in sharp angles, as in triangular plots of land, it is believed that the energy will be trapped in the corners, and will become stagnant. However, there are innumerable Feng Shui cures (pages 76–93) that will help stimulate the flow of energy in even the most inauspicious of gardens.

Triangular properties relate to the Fire element (page 24), and can imbue an area with unstable energy, both wildly positive and dramatically negative. Although circular properties are rare, sometimes a house and garden are perched on a slightly domed hill; they will then attract the energy of Metal (page 21).

Irregularly shaped properties are symbolic of the energy of Water (page 22). This leads to the generation of an unstable flow of qi, but it can be "cured" by disguising all the protruding corners as "garden rooms."

Below: The yin and yang symbol is an important basis of Feng Shui – the constant need to find and maintain balance. Incorporate the concept of balance in the way you approach your garden and home and you will experience major, satisfying changes in life.

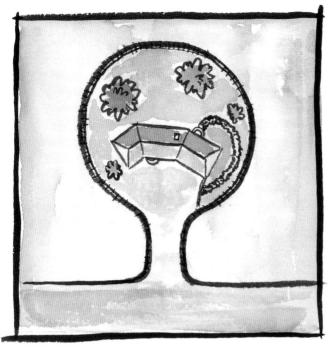

Circular Plot

Irregular Plot

Triangular Plot

Rectangular Plot

The effect of your surroundings

Above: Chinese "moon" windows are an excellent way of framing a garden scene beyond a wall and allowing the energy to harmoniously flow through, attracted by the pleasant view. Unlike rectangular or square frames, circular windows do not create poison arrows.

The impact of your surroundings is very important to the flow of energy in your property. A pleasant scene in the distance, the position of a school or cemetery, the local street plan – all these have a tremendous effect on your life and important ramifications for what you need to do in your garden to enhance or counterbalance these environmental features.

For instance, if you have a pleasant view or scenery in the distance, use the plantings in the garden to "frame" the view, incorporating the scenery into your garden design. Views of gentle hills with a stream or creek at the base, or of serene woods or forests, are believed to provide a flow of lucky energy.

However, views of mountains can be overwhelming if they rise above eye level in the distance. Mountains and their energy flow beneficially if they are flowing from the north and east, or if they are positioned at, or seen from, the back of the house or property. To counterbalance any overwhelming energy from a mountain range, hang a mirror in the largest window facing the mountains or position it on the fence facing the mountains.

Other disruptive energies can flow from a westerly direction. To balance this energy, install garden lighting or, a still water feature. Be sure to keep the water clean at all times. Do not hang any chimes in this area – the sounds created may arouse the energy of the tiger, adding to the flow of negative disruptive energy.

Assess the position of trees both on your property and in the area immediately around your property. It is considered particularly unlucky if a tree is planted in front of the entrance to your property or your front door. This can cause conflict and tension to enter your garden and home, as the tree interferes with the flow of lucky energy into your space and life. Either get permission to remove the tree or plant a protective hedge to filter the effect of the poison arrow.

Similarly, if a telephone pole is creating poison arrows aimed at your property (for example, if the pole is sited directly opposite your front door), plant a protective screen, install a lattice panel or position a mirror to reflect the poison arrow back toward the base of the pole or tree.

The position of other buildings and sites around you can also project excessive yang and yin energy that will need to be counterbalanced. Strong yang energy is projected by schools, colleges, train stations, airports – any place where there is an excessive flow of traffic. To counterbalance this flow of energy, use protective screen plantings of dense green shrubbery or install a water feature.

Strong yin energy emanates from cemeteries, churches, police stations and any other buildings where pain and suffering is felt, including hospitals and nursing homes. As this is an extremely passive energy, place objects that generate movement and sound in areas facing these types of buildings – wooden mobiles, wind chimes or bamboo flutes. Consider installing a feature corresponding to the Fire (yang) element, such as garden lighting. The best solution is to incorporate nine red lights in the area.

The local street plan around your property also affects the flow of energy to your property. Plant or install protective screenings or install a water feature if you live at a T intersection and the road is aimed directly at your house.

Below left: High, straight walls, while useful in screening your house and garden from negative energy of various forms, may itself create fast-running poison arrows along its straight edges. To counterbalance the creation of such energy, plant shrubs, trees and flowers along the wall to soften the flow of energy.

Below center: The view of the garden from the french doors and top window of the house will help enhance the flow of energy through the house, as well as in the garden.

Below right: Avoid planting trees in front of paths and major entrances – confine them to areas where they can enhance the flow of energy rather than hinder it.

What are the eight aspirations in Feng Shui?

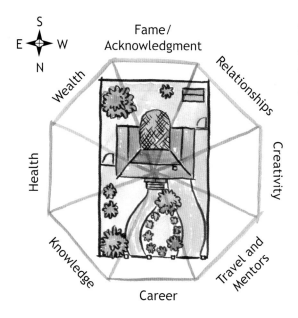

Above: The bagua is shown here superimposed on a residential site according to the compass reading taken.

Opposite: A garden can be constructed and planted so that the flow of beneficial energy is enhanced in all eight aspirations.

The eight aspirations are the eight most important aspects of your life that can be affected by the flow of energy in your space. The aspirations are wealth, fame, health, creativity, mentors, knowledge, relationships and career. In Feng Shui, each aspiration corresponds to a compass direction:

Compass direction	Aspiration
North	Career
South	Fame, acknowledgment and promotion
East	Family and health
West	Children and creativity
Northwest	Mentors, useful friends in authority, travel
Northeast	Knowledge and study
Southwest	Relationships
Southeast	Wealth and prosperity

Using the bagua template that you have already drawn for your home and garden or separate gardens (pages 28–29), mark the eight aspirations on the eight segments of the circle.

It is believed that the strategic positioning of certain garden ornaments, objects, and plants can enhance any of these aspirations. If you are feeling lonely and unsupported, for instance, there are ways of improving this state of affairs by focusing on the relationships or mentors section of your garden. Pages 36–45 will give some suggestions on how to enhance these areas of your life.

Above: It is important that the water in a pond is always kept fresh and clean. Having fish in your pond will help keep the water clear of certain algae and will keep the water in constant motion.

Above: Bamboo is symbolic of Wood, an element that is nurtured by Water. Plant or keep a potted bamboo plant in the Wealth sector to generate a sense of prosperity and abundance.

Improving prosperity

The prosperity area of your garden corresponds to a southeasterly direction. Check this area for poison arrows and implement strategies to soften or screen the area if the object or feature creating those poison arrows cannot be removed.

The next thing to do is to remove any clutter or dead trees from this area. Dead trees generate an extremely yin energy, reminiscent of winter energy. Your money resources will always seem to disappear (going underground like the energy of winter) if there is too much yin energy present.

Whenever you remove a tree from a particular area, assess why the tree died and, if appropriate, plant something else in the area that is more suitable for the soil and the amount of sun or shade there. After removing the tree, work on improving the soil and wait a while – for the energy to rebalance – before replanting.

In Feng Shui, wealth corresponds to the element of Water. It is always wise to incorporate a pond, pool, birdbath or other water feature in this area of the garden, to enhance the flow of wealth in the family. If you have a pond or a pool, make sure it is in good condition and that the water is kept clean; also make sure that any taps in this area do not leak.

In Feng Shui, it is considered an excellent boost to success and wealth if you keep an even number of goldfish or koi in your pond – the golden sheen of their scales has been often used to symbolize theflow of success and wealth into the home.

Use objects and plants that correspond to the element of Water (page 22) and Metal (page 21) in this area to improve the energy for this aspiration. Remove objects that correspond to Fire (page 24).

Feng Shui garden tip
Plant some golden clumping bamboo in the southeast to help nurture your financial prospects.

Getting the acknowledgment you deserve

Feng Shui garden tip

To stimulate acknowledgment energy, place a fresh red flower from your garden in a small, light-colored glass vase on your desk at work or in your home office so that it is near the top middle part of the desk. Remove the flower just before it begins to wilt.

The fame, acknowledgment and promotion area of the garden corresponds to the southerly direction. This area also relates to the element of Fire (page 24). Check this area for poison arrows, and if there are any, implement strategies to soften or screen their energy.

Include a Fire plant or object in this area and consider using solar-powered lighting here. Place your barbecues, ovens and outdoor heating in this area. An increase in the level of lighting in this area acts like neon lights around your name in terms of fame and acknowledgment. Soon you will feel as if you are being noticed. Include red candles, decorator lanterns made of red glass or pretty Christmas tree lights in suitable trees or shrubs around the barbecue.

An attractive feature in this part of the garden would be a small garden bed featuring a specimen red flowering plant, such as California poppies or dahlias (plants that flower in summer, the season that corresponds to Fire). Surround the flower feature with plants that resonate with the element of Wood, such as a boxwood hedge, and incorporate a reflective surface, such as silver or gold colored pebbles or a cluster of stainless steel balls, among the plants.

Right: Lighting and red-colored flowers or berries are an excellent way of stimulating the energy of your fame and acknowledgment aspiration, especially if this area is planted with dark foliage or if it is often in the shade.

Improving your love life

Above: The yang energy of red flowers can help stimulate the most sluggish of relationships. Plant them in the relationship area of your garden and tend them well. Be careful not to place too many yang features in this area – remember that you must always have balance in your garden.

Opposite: Statues of happy couples should be included in your relationship area. It is important to have an even number of statues or figures in a group statue. Avoid statues where the figures imply some form of distress or grief, such as the bust of a woman with her face hidden by a veil.

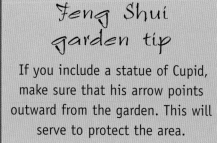

Feng Shui garden tip

If you include a statue of Cupid, make sure that his arrow points outward from the garden. This will serve to protect the area.

If you are feeling unloved or unhappy in a dead-end relationship, or have suffered a string of unsatisfying relationships, you can make changes in this aspect of your life by improving the relationships area of your garden. The relationships aspect of life corresponds to the southwesterly direction.

Use softening or screening strategies if this area of the garden is subject to poison arrows and then clear the area of clutter – overgrown weeds in the garden beds, unkempt pathways, poor growth in the garden bed, unwanted boxes, piles of trash or debris.

Also clear this area of dead trees or straggly plants. Keep any lawn in this area mown and in good condition, and concentrate on improving the soil, so that you will generate healthy growth in the area.

If you have been feeling lonely, check that this section of the garden, particularly in the front yard, is not too yin in energy. If this area is in constant shade and there is a sense of stagnation, your relationships may suffer from a similar feeling of stagnation, and perhaps too much introspection. If you cut back any overgrowth and let more sunlight into this area, you will feel a marked improvement in this aspect of your life.

However, if the area is too yang (the garden beds have dried out, there is not enough shade or the ground is too stony and dry, for instance), you may find that your relationships are too demanding and tiring. If you plant more trees in this area to give shade, and perhaps add more mulch or humus to the soil, you will allow more harmonizing energy into this aspect of your life.

Fruit trees, such as cherry and apple trees, can be included in this area to generate a literally "fruitful" relationship. In Feng Shui, it is believed that planting or placing objects in pairs encourages a harmonious love energy.

By implementing these simple strategies, you will be helping to clear the negative energies that have been clouding your love life. To ensure a change of luck in this aspect, install a pair of statues, such as a pair of doves, mandarin ducks or lovers, in this area.

Above: Peaceful, contemplative statues help anchor creative energy and allow you to harness it for your creative projects. Choose a statue that resonates with your creative venture; for example, if you have to do some writing, put an image of Saint Luke or Wen Ch'ang in this area as these figures resonate with writing and literature.

Enhancing creativity

Energies that affect creativity and the aspect of children in your life come from the westerly direction. Although the energy from this direction can be unsettled, once it is stabilized it can be effectively harnessed to help you either further your creativity or harmonize the energy of your children.

It is important not to disturb or activate this westerly energy. Place only quiet, still objects, such as a statue or some heavy, rounded rocks, in the western sector of your garden. The statue should be made of an earthy substance – earthenware or terracotta – but it can also be made of metal, such as steel or bronze.

The west resonates with the element of Metal (page 21), so a suitable feature would be a stone sculpture; something that is full of rounded lines, and that represents a peaceful subject, such as a person in contemplation (pages 58–59).

As usual, check this area for poison arrows and clear away any clutter, overgrown plants and dead trees or shrubs. You could even place the sculpture so that it deflects the poison arrows.

Consider incorporating plants and objects that resonate with Metal and the supportive element of Earth (page 20).

An attractive feature would be a rock garden full of plants that resonate with Earth, such as fragrant herbs and ground cover plants, and plants that have orange and yellow flowers. At the top of the rock garden place a statue and plant a rounded/dome-shaped tree.

Left: Make sure that the rocks you use do not have jagged edges. Use only those that are fully rounded or that have their surfaces softened by moss. Interspersing the rocks with dense, rounded shrubs will further help soften any stray sharp edges.

Finding helpful people

The aspiration that governs the acquisition of friends, the support of influential people in authority, and the meeting of important people through your travels is governed by northwesterly energy. This energy is also helpful for people seeking spiritual help and succor.

If you are finding that people in authority are overlooking you or your work, check that this northwesterly area of the garden is not the target of any poison arrows. Also ensure that the fame and acknowledgment area of your garden is in good condition (page 37).

The energy in this area resonates with the time of early winter. It is an energy that is starting to move deep underground. To honor and strengthen this energy, you may wish to plant a garden that will flower at the beginning of winter. This kind of garden will need to include a number of frost-resistant plants, such as certain evergreens and bulbs.

Include objects of metal or stone – perhaps statues of spiritual leaders, such as Buddha, Jesus Christ, the Virgin Mary, and the holy saints, or of mentors, such as Roman senators or Greek philosophers. Your statue can be positioned so that it deflects a poison arrow entering this area.

Consider scattering some reflective silver or gold colored pebbles among the plants to evoke an atmosphere of success.

Above: Turn the mentor segment of your garden into a lush, quiet arbor where you can sit and contemplate the friendships and mentors you have known. Make sure that access to this area is easy and flows in gentle curves.

Feng Shui garden tip

Statues carrying weapons are best avoided unless placed near the gate or main door of the home to stand as protectors. Statues of heroes represent positive aspiration and are particularly effective in the northwest area of the garden.

Right: Plantings that are golden in color or trees whose leaves turn golden in autumn will enhance the mentor aspiration if planted in the northwesterly section of your garden.

Strengthening your career path

The career aspiration corresponds to the northerly direction. This energy is a nurturing one, and is symbolized in Chinese philosophies as the mythical Celestial Black Tortoise. After assessing this section of the garden for poison arrows, implementing strategies to soften or screen this negative energy and removing clutter and debris from this area, incorporate a small image of a turtle or tortoise.

Tuck this little image, whether it's a small statue or a waterproof drawing, beside your back door or by a water feature in this northerly area, and make sure it is facing north. This image will strengthen the flow of good luck to you and will help you find work that will harmonize with your character.

Black is a yin color, and symbolizes the yin quality of this area, in contrast with the southerly yang energy of Fire. This northerly part of the garden is an introspective area, which also relates to the element of Water (page 22) and the energy of winter (page 97).

Be careful that this section is not overly yin in energy, as this will indicate difficulties in moving forward in your career. If there is too much shade, consider moving some of the plants – too many plants in the area may be draining the nurturing energy, as well as adding to the yin energy. Similarly, in your career, you may find that you feel overworked.

You need to be careful with replanting and pruning: Feng Shui principles do not support disturbing the flow of nature by too much replanting or pruning that will damage the plant.

As well as allowing more sunlight into this area, you may also add objects that represent movement. Hang a mobile from a tree or string some colorful flags across a balustrade or a porch, or from tree to tree. These objects will pick up and enhance the movement of the wind and qi through this area of the garden, similarly improving the flow of energy around your career.

As this area corresponds to Water, include plants and objects that resonate with this element, as well as the supportive element of Metal (page 21). However, remove or avoid incorporating plants and objects that resonate with the element of Earth (page 20).

Above: The yang energy of red flowers will stimulate the career sector of your garden, but be sure to balance the colors on display by including the milder shades, such as pinks, oranges and yellows.

Opposite, clockwise from top left: Metal sculptures near a water feature will harmonize the flow of energy; hanging a wind chime will enhance the movement of qi in this area; clean, clear rippling water is a symbol of wealth and is an auspicious element to add to your career sector, and adding turtles or tortoises to your water feature will generate good luck.

Helping your studies

The acquisition of knowledge, and success in your studies, corresponds to the northeasterly direction. In this area of the garden, the nurturing energy of the north combines with the energy of the east, an energy that resonates with wisdom and culture.

If you are feeling blocked and always tired when you are studying, check whether this area is too yin in energy. This area may feel stagnant and cluttered, echoing your feelings of being overwhelmed by the amount of study you have to do. The first step is to clear this area of the garden.

As this area corresponds to the element of Earth, enhance this area with plants and objects that correspond to the Earth and Fire elements (pages 20 and 24), such as crystals.

Feelings of tiredness and overwork may also occur if this area is subject to an overly yang energy, particularly if the area is very dry, rocky and sunny. Take some breaks during your studies to work on this area and improve the soil. As this area corresponds with the symbol of the mountain, consider creating a mound to represent a mountain.

Create a space in this area where you can refresh yourself and tune into the harmonious flow of nature. You could make an attractive feature here by setting up a display of colorful plants and shrubs – particularly those with red, orange or yellow flowers – around an elevated sculpture or lantern that resonates with the shape of a pagoda to attract good luck and success in your exams.

Above and left: Beds of red, orange and yellow flowers and water trickling down a rocky slope will refresh your mind as well as your soul.

Improving your health

The aspiration that relates to your health and the flow of harmony among your family members corresponds to the area of your garden that faces east. If you are constantly experiencing health problems, concentrate on improving the garden in this area.

Place an image or a wooden sculpture of a dragon in this area, and surround it with plants and objects that correspond to the element of Wood (page 23), such as a pergola and or an arbor. Make sure that the image is a peaceful one and the dragon does not appear to be fierce.

Dragons are traditionally placed in the eastern part of the garden. However, they can also be positioned to counterbalance any powerful negative energy aimed at your garden or home.

Counteract any poison arrows aimed at this eastern section, and the area by your bedroom window, to help improve the flow of a healthy energy to you.

An attractive feature in this area would be a wooden arbor surrounding a statue of a dragon with a backdrop of living bamboo. Bamboo is an excellent symbol of the energy of Wood and there are many non-invasive varieties – look for smaller, clump-forming varieties or slow-growing varieties, such as Shibataea lancifolia.

Above right: Bamboo is symbolic of longevity and is believed to be helpful in distributing beneficial energy.

Right: The dragon is one of the Celestial animals that represent the four points of the compass – the dragon is symbolic of the wisdom of the east.

Above: Curved paths and hedges planted to cover sharp edges are an important part of Feng Shui design in the garden.

Above: Weathered steps and rounded moldings help the flow of beneficial energy.

Opposite: The entrance to this path is marked by two rounded evergreen hedges that encourage the gentle flow of energy along the curved path through the garden.

Harmonizing with nature

The key to attracting beneficial energy into your garden and into your life is to tune into the flow of nature. In Feng Shui, this is done by harmonizing with the cycle of the seasons, which is related to the flow of energies from the north, south, west and east, and to the energies created by the five elements of Earth, Metal, Wood, Fire, and Water.

From the interrelationships of these various energy forms and through the observations of Feng Shui practitioners over the centuries, various ways of encouraging the flow of beneficial energy through an area have been devised, affecting what we should place in our garden and home and where these objects and plants should be positioned.

Two of the most important areas to focus on in the garden are the entrance to the garden and to the house (pages 48–49). It is extremely important that these areas are harmonious in terms of proportion, design, and color. Use your intuition and your own taste to make these areas pleasant and attractive.

Feng Shui garden tip

If you have a main gate, make sure it looks inviting and well maintained, and make sure it opens inward (into the garden).

An excellent rule of thumb in Feng Shui is that energy will flow beneficially in any area that looks pleasing and well cared for. All structures, ornaments, furniture and other garden objects must be kept clean, clear of debris and in good working order. These Feng Shui principles should also be applied to features of the garden, such as paths, statues, fountains, and lighting. You also need to give special consideration to the types of plants that can be used to screen or enhance the flow of energy through the garden.

The entrance

The entrance to your garden and the path leading to the front door of your home should be one of your first concerns when focusing on making your garden a new haven for the beneficial flow of positive energy.

Stand at the entrance to your garden and assess how the energy is reaching your garden entrance. Energy usually flows to a property along the road, generally in the direction of the traffic on your side of the street. This energy flows beneficially if the street curves, reflecting the gentle flow of a river or stream. On streets that are straight, the qi moves too fast; it can be slowed down by planting trees and shrubs along the street.

As front boundary lines and our fences are generally in a straight line, it is important to plant along the outside of the fence, particularly if it is a solid stone, timber or brick wall that does not allow qi to filter through. Set out curved garden beds along your fence line using low-growing fragrant plants and herbs, such as lavender, scented geraniums and some species of thornless roses, to attract the flow of qi to your front garden entrance.

If you don't have a fence, plant some shrubs and trees in natural clumps across the front of your garden. Proportion is very important in Feng Shui:

Feng Shui garden tip

Your front entrance (of either your house or garden) should, ideally, face moving water, which should be installed at a minimum distance of 10 feet (3 meters) from the front door.

Right: The energy flows to this front door over a bridge and across a series of softly rectangular pavers to the front door. The gravel between the pavers further softens the shape of the paving. Do not let the path to the front door meander too much otherwise you may arrive at your front door feeling too tired.

if the entrance to the garden or the house is too large, the energy that enters may be in the form of sha qi. The literal translation of sha qi is "killing breath," and it travels in straight lines. Sha qi is an overwhelming energy that brings with it overtiredness, ill health, and headaches; however, if there is only a tiny entrance to your garden, too little energy will make its way into the front yard and your home will be too yin, generating introspection and little luck or sense of success.

Next, assess how the energy is flowing through the garden to the front door. Walk through the garden in the way you usually use to get to the front door. Are there any straight lines? You may already have a meandering path to your front door, which is ideal.

If the path is straight, redesign it so that it has a gentle curve (pages 50–51) or, if you can't replace it immediately, try softening the edges with fragrant plantings, such as lavender, heliotrope, hyacinths or carpet roses, and plant some ground cover plants along the edges so that they will encroach upon the edges of the path. Again choose fragrant ground cover plants such as prostrate rosemary, verbena, and thyme.

Avoid planting roses anywhere along this important path to your front door: according to Feng Shui principles, the thorns will snag the energy flowing into your home, and from a practical point of view, the thorns will snag the clothes of you, your family and your guests.

Below left: Using rounded pots and growing shrubs that can be gently pruned into rounded shapes can help de-emphasize rectangular pavers.

Below center: The curve of this beautifully planted garden helps the energy flow slowly and beneficially towards the front door, which is flanked by square, straight yang-style columns. The curve of the garden path helps balance the rectangular entrance.

Below right: Using flowers and plantings to de-emphasize the rectangular features of modern Western homes can improve the flow of energy into such homes.

Paths and pavements

Assess all the paths in your garden and soften any straight outlines – Feng Shui says that energy flows beneficially in curves and detrimentally in straight lines. To assure yourself that changing the shape of your path is a very important step towards creating a harmonious garden, one that is good for your soul and the progress of your life, make a note of what happens at the end of a straight path.

Straight path checklist

At the end of a straight path, have you noticed any of the following:

1. Clutter or garden debris?   Yes   No
2. A dead or dying plant?   Yes   No
3. A garden structure in poor repair?   Yes   No
4. Arguments and disagreements flaring up?   Yes   No

If you have answered "yes" to any of the above questions, make reshaping the straight path a priority in your gardening schedule.

Above: A curved path of irregular-shaped flagstones that is further softened by low and varied plantings is considered good Feng Shui.

Opposite: Curved paths help counterbalance straight elements in the garden, such as mature trees with a section of bare trunk or garden ornament features.

There are many types of paths – concrete, brick paving, timber, gravel and grass, for example. Generally, in Western garden design, it is believed that only one type of path should be used in the garden, to give a sense of unity to the design. In the East, garden paths are usually covered with a variety of different types of materials.

One of the cheapest and most useful types of pathway is one filled with gravel. Gravel paths allow some flexibility in terms of changing and rearranging your garden – you can easily expand garden beds and create paths that lead to newly cultivated sites, for instance. Although gravel paths require maintenance, such as raking and occasional weeding, they have a security benefit, as walking on them creates a great deal of noise.

If you wish to be adventurous in your garden design, you could consider choosing the materials for your paths according to the direction each path is traveling in. For instance, a path that leads to a garden shed situated in the north of your garden corresponds to the element of Water, which is nurtured by Metal. Use a series of white, circular stepping-stones for this path.

Apart from the shape and material of the path, remember that the aspect of the path, the look of it as you move along it, must always be pleasant. Even if a path is curved, still consider planting low-growing shrubs and fragrant flowers and herbs along it to encourage the energy to flow beneficially. Fragrant herbs such as lavender, rosemary, and thyme are popular edgings. You could also experiment with using metal, wood or another material to edge the path so that it is distinctly separate from the rest of the garden but still corresponds to the direction that it is heading in. This principle can also be applied to the edging of garden beds situated in a particular compass direction.

Direction	Corresponding element and color	Corresponding type of path	Corresponding garden edging
Center Southwest Northeast	Earth (page 20) Yellow and brown	Gravel, brick or stone paving	Brick, stone or molded terracotta edgings
West Northwest	Metal (page 21) White and silver	White gravel, brick or stone paving	Brick, stone or pressed metal edgings
North	Water (page 22) Blue and black	Bluestone paving	Pressed metal edgings
East Southeast	Wood (page 23) Green	Decking, brick or stone	Timber, brick or stone edgings
South	Fire (page 24) Red	Decking	Timber edgings

Plantings to attract beneficial energy

Above: Hydrangeas help complement the curve to this path, which is made of a series of bricks. The edges have been softened by the growth of moss in between the bricks.

Opposite: The rounded shapes of the plantings are complemented by the rounded water feature tucked into a corner of the garden. Remember to balance dark yin-like foliage with highlights of yang-colored flowers, such as reds, pinks, and yellows.

The shape of plants can attract certain types of energy into a garden and into your life. Use the following table to see the correspondences between plant shapes, compass directions and the five Chinese elements:

Direction	Corresponding element	Corresponding shapes and lines
Center Southwest Northeast	Earth (page 20)	Square
West Northwest	Metal (page 21)	Circle
North	Water (page 22)	Undulating line
East Southeast	Wood (page 23)	Rectangle
South	Fire (page 24)	Triangle

Each type of plant shape can be used in the corresponding direction in the garden to enhance the flow of the energy from that particular direction (pages 18–25). This is particularly useful if you have a blockage of energy from a certain direction. For instance, if the view is unpleasant from your easterly direction, blocking energy that attracts culture and wisdom, plant rectangular plants. To achieve a sense of harmony, health and balance in a home and garden it is imperative to have a balance of the energies of all the elements.

However, it is also important to choose an effective way of enhancing beneficial energy from a particular direction. If some of the plants suggested will not thrive in a certain direction in your garden, consider incorporating one of the many Feng Shui cures (pages 76–93) and other garden Feng Shui strategies, such as planting flowers or shrubs that flower in a color that corresponds to the elemental energy you wish to attract.

To enhance the flow of energy from the southwest or northeast, which corresponds to the flow of stable and life-enhancing qi, plant square plants such as yew trees, use a garden edging of boxwood or fill a garden bed with California poppy or verbena. To harness the flow of energy from the west and northwest, plant circular plants such as hydrangeas and chives. Rounded shapes also manifest in some trees – the oak tree, for instance, and weeping plants of different varieties, such as the willow. To encourage the flow of energy from the east and southeast, plant rectangular plants such as dogwood and certain cypresses.

To enhance the flow of energy from the south, which is believed to be lucky, plant triangular plants, such as beeches, some evergreen conifers (do not plant trees that will eventually be very large and block the flow of this energy), ferns and irises. To enhance the flow of nurturing energy from the north, plant trees and shrubs that have undulating or wavy shapes, such as honeysuckle, wisteria and rhododendrons.

Feng Shui garden tip

Keep trees at a distance from the house to avoid root damage to the building, which may lead to corresponding cracks occurring in the occupants' lives. Ideally, trees should be planted at such a distance that they do not cast a shadow on the house when they are fully matured (for example, if a tree grows to 26 feet [8 meters], plant it at least 26 feet from the house).

Trees, hedges and screens

In Feng Shui, trees, hedges and screens are very useful in screening either poison arrows created by features in the environment, garden or structures, or unfavorable energy created by inauspicious views from your house or any other inauspicious features in your garden.

If you have already identified that the energy from one direction is unfavorable, choose a tree, hedge or other screen that corresponds to the energy of that direction in terms of either color (pages 18–25) or shape (pages 52–53).

Choose your screens according to where they need to be placed in the garden. In the north, choose screens made from metal; in the south, use timber; in the west, use a brick wall (made from bricks laid with spaces between them) or a metal lattice or wire fence; in the east, use a timber lattice or a woven fence.

Overall, fragrant trees and hedges, or those with attractively colored leaves or flowers, are the best types of plants for screening negative energy of any sort. One kind of attractive hedge can be made with a repeated planting of abelia, camellia, hibiscus, honeysuckle and orange jasmine.

In some Feng Shui systems, the energy of certain trees in a garden resonates with certain members of your family. This is one reason that pruning is treated with caution in Feng Shui. To prune a tree is seen as akin to pruning the growth and potential of a person – your child or spouse, perhaps – and it is therefore thought to bring bad luck. However, the healthy growth of a plant is often dependent on some pruning. Similarly, children (or, indeed, adults) will not develop to their full potential if they are not given some rules and boundaries to observe.

The solution is to find a balance between growth (yang) and pruning (a yin activity). Consequently, prune and deadhead plants when they need it, and only prune what is absolutely required to keep the plant in good shape and condition. This means you will need to be doing some regular maintenance of your garden. The more plants you have, the more time you need to spend to keep them in good condition.

Below: Timber screens are best chosen for the south or east side of your garden. Lattices are an excellent form of protection because the structure still allows for energy to flow.

In Eastern gardens, the concept of "overplanting" (overfilling garden beds with plants and flowers) is not encouraged. Rather, a few beautiful specimen plants are incorporated in a garden design, creating optimal balance between yang features (plants, rocks and structures) and yin space.

The following are areas where protective planting and screening would benefit the flow of energy in the garden:

- at the end of a long corridor (such as the area between the fence and the house);
- at the end of a long, straight path or garden bed;
- where there is an unpleasant view or in an area which contains an overly yin or yang type of building or site (such as a church or power lines – pages 14–15); and
- the corners of your house (and, if you can see your neighbor's house, the corners and roofline of that house as well).

Below left: Leafy, bamboo screening is best used to balance overly yang areas that are too sunny and dry. It is thought to be lucky to have potted bamboo screens near the front of the house.

Below center: If you do not want to grow bamboo in your garden, even in pots, consider using lightweight bamboo screens in the areas that need screening.

Below right: Lattices painted in yang colors, such as red, orange, pink or yellow, teamed with yang-colored foliage or flowers, can be used as screens near water features in the garden.

> ## Feng Shui garden tip
>
> Make sure that the screening plants on your front boundary line do not grow higher than 3 feet (1 meter) in height. Otherwise, qi will not flow as beneficially.

Water features

According to Feng Shui principles, a water feature must be incorporated in the garden to encourage the flow of beneficial energy. The best positions for a water feature are in the areas that correspond to the wealth, career and family/health sectors of the garden. These are the southeasterly, northerly and easterly parts of the garden, respectively.

The water feature can be anything from a birdbath to an elaborate waterfall or a wall fountain. It must be rounded in shape, preferably either circular or kidney-shaped, and the edges can be planted with shrubs or flowers that correspond to the Metal element (page 21).

It is important that the pool looks as natural as possible. There are many ornate fountains that work well in a formal garden; however, in Feng Shui, the emphasis is on moving away from traditional formal garden designs that use symmetrical square or rectangular garden beds and towards landscaped gardens that echo the flow of the yin and yang symbol. A predominance of artificial materials in a garden, such as plastics and concrete, will not help generate the flow of good energy.

It is important to keep all water features in the garden in good repair and not to allow stagnation to creep in. It is believed that water draining or dripping away, especially into the earth, evokes a destructive energy between the elements, which then becomes an unlucky or inauspicious flow of energy in your garden and your life. In Feng Shui, it is believed that such leaks and disrepair will be reflected in financial problems, particularly the feeling that your money seems to just disappear.

Other auspicious positions for a water feature in your garden are in the front yard, near your front entrance, particularly if the view from the front door is not particularly pleasant or if a poison arrow hits the front door. Also, you can install a wall fountain on the wall of your house.

If you have a swimming pool in your back yard, an area that is already yin in energy, you run the risk of creating an overly yin energy in this private area. The solution is to incorporate more yang energy objects – a garden structure such as an attractive bathhouse or pergola, perhaps, which you can use as a changing room or a place to rest in after a swim (see also page 58).

Above and opposite: The sound of running water will help you feel relaxed and can help clear negative energy from the garden as well as your life. Water features should either look natural (above) or be rounded in shape (opposite). The path around or near the water feature should allow the energy to arrive or flow around the feature in gentle, easy curves.

Feng Shui garden tip

If you are installing a swimming pool, make sure that the design is in proportion with the house and the property.

Garden statues

Above: Garden statues are very useful for counteracting poison arrows; for example, those that are created by a corner in the garden edging.

Opposite: Place your garden statuary in auspicious positions. One such position includes placing a light-colored statue among dark foliage, balancing the yin energy of the foliage with the yang energy of the statue.

Feng Shui garden tip

Statues that represent positive aspirations foster good Feng Shui and should be placed insuch a way that the energies they generate are subtle.

Garden statues of dragons in the easterly part of your garden, a phoenix in the south and a tortoise in the north invoke the energy, respectively, of wisdom, good luck and nurture. Statues that represent yang energy, such as dragons, are best placed in shady areas to balance the yin energy of the space, while yin energy statues (for example, those where the image is in a meditative pose) are best placed in sunny, dry areas of the garden.

The tiger of the west is rarely incorporated into the garden, as this creature represents a potentially disruptive energy that really needs to be left alone and not disturbed. However, its image can be used as a symbol of protection if it looks benign rather than aggressive.

This westerly energy can be stabilized with heavy objects. For example, use a garden statue that represents calm and wisdom, such as the image of a seated Buddha.

Incorporating important spiritual figures in any aspect of the garden is considered auspicious as long as the images are treated with honor and respect. Do not place images of Buddha or the popular goddess of compassion, Kuan Yin, anywhere near a sewage outlet or the compost heap.

These statues should be placed in areas of honor – for instance, on a ledge or pedestal above the ground in a space that is seen as soon as a person enters that section of the garden (a position similar to the "honored guest" position in the dining room – the "honored guest" is the first person you see as you enter the room.)

Incorporate an image of a frog with your pond to stimulate further good luck for any of your financial ventures. If you have a large water feature in your garden, such as a swimming pool, consider placing a statue of a dragon turtle between the pool and your house.

A dragon turtle has the head of a dragon and the body of a turtle, and is an excellent Feng Shui cure (see also pages 76–93), counterbalancing the overly yin energy created by the pool. Similarly, if your house faces a huge body of water, such as a water reservoir, place the statue in front of your house so that it is facing the water feature.

Garden ornaments

Above: Garden ornaments are also useful in helping move beneficial energy along a lengthy meandering pathway.

Right: In dark, shady areas of your garden, possibly tucked away from the main garden, include a brightly colored garden ornament to balance the yin energy of the spot and create an aesthetically pleasing tableau, which will help generate good energy and add to the power of the beneficial energy already circulating around the garden.

Garden ornaments are fun ways of improving the flow of beneficial energy through the garden. Nestled among the plants, such garden ornaments as pyramid-shaped garden stakes, birdhouses and feeders, mirror balls and colorful mosaics can add interest and stimulation to various parts of the garden where the energy is moving a little too slowly, causing stagnation and clutter.

You do not need to use specifically oriental ornaments, statues and other garden features to create a Feng Shui garden. You can easily encourage the flow of beneficial energy around you by using ordinary garden ornaments. Just take care to follow the basic principles of Feng Shui concerning the balance between yin and yang (pages 14–15) and the elements (pages 18–25). For example, position a playful grouping of colorful birdhouses in the middle of some dense green foliage.

In the south part of your garden, use objects that are spiky or triangular, such as birdhouses, to add the energy of Fire (page 24) to the space. Other ordinary garden ornaments that resonate with the element of Fire include pyramid-shaped garden stakes for holding up plants that need support, such as tomatoes. However, be careful to avoid sharply angled decorations, such as weather vanes or square planters for trees that won't be covered or softened by plants.

Metal garden ornaments, such as stainless steel metal balls and flat metal silhouettes of fairies or other mythical creatures, can be placed in either the northwest or the west. Metal sculptures of frogs or cranes complement the energy of water features, which are often beneficially placed in the north.

As with the use of Feng Shui cures to balance the flow of energy in a space (pages 76–93), do not overuse garden ornaments in your garden, as this may lead to the area feeling cluttered and over stimulated.

Other garden ornaments include water features (pages 56–57), garden statues (pages 58–59), outdoor furniture (pages 62–63), garden structures (pages 64–65) and lighting (pages 66–67). Also consider placing flags, mobiles, and other Feng Shui cures that move with the wind in your garden to create interest and to stimulate the movement of beneficial energy (page 93).

Outdoor furniture

As the garden is being used more and more as an extension of the house, the placement of outdoor furniture in newly created "garden rooms" needs to follow some of the same Feng Shui rules that apply to the placement of furniture inside your home.

For instance, when positioning a seat or a swing in the garden or on the porch, make sure that the back of the seat or swing is not facing an opening to that garden area, or a side street, or the entrance to the porch. Similarly, when you hang a swing, either in the garden for the children or on the porch, make sure that its back is not facing an opening, such as a doorway or a gate. For children, this will help reduce the chance of accidents occurring, as they will not feel vulnerable and restless swinging with their back toward the main flow of energy into the area where the swing is.

Also take into consideration the harmonies between the elements. For example, you can place a wooden garden seat around a tree that is shaped like a square, representing the element of Earth, as this element is of no threat to Wood. However, do not place a wooden seat around a plant that represents the element of Metal, such as a weeping plant, or one that is circular in shape, as Metal is detrimental to Wood.

Wooden furniture is auspiciously placed in the east, southeast and south; metal furniture is best placed in the north, northwest or west. However, if the energy from the west is already too disruptive, consider placing metal furniture only in the north or northwest. Also, pieces of metal furniture are best placed by a stone wall or near a water feature.

Pieces of stone furniture resonate with the element of Earth and are best positioned in the center of the garden or in the southwest or northeast. In a formal garden, a centrally placed stone seat anchoring the energy of the garden with the element of Earth would be a harmonious setting. Make sure that the seat has its back protected – with dense green shrubs, for instance.

As mentioned before, avoid using pieces of furniture that are not made of wood, stone or metal in the garden. Artificial substances, such as vinyl or plastic, are best avoided in the garden.

Outdoor dining will be even more harmonious if you make sure that the table is oval or circular and that there is an even number of chairs. It is important that no chair back faces the main entrance into the outdoor dining space. Seat your guests in the "honored guest" positions – so that they are facing the entrance to the dining space.

If you are dining under a pergola, make sure that the rafters or roof battens are covered for the evening with, for example, a pretty piece of all-weather cloth.

Similarly, do not hang a hammock between two posts of a pergola, as the beam above you will "cut" you in half. You will have a much better rest if the hammock is tied between two trees where there are no branches, or at most a few branches, above you.

> ## Feng Shui garden tip
>
> Good Feng Shui requires that objects be clean and in good working order. Make sure that furniture in exposed parts of the garden is well maintained. Repair broken chairs and discard damaged pots and containers.

Below left: As much as possible, outdoor wooden furniture and arbors should be constructed from rounded planks and supports.

Below center: Wicker furniture, which can be woven so that there are no sharp edges, resonates with the element of Wood.

Below right: Use round columns as supports when designing pergolas and other garden structures. In Feng Shui, it is believed that sharp-edged objects, such as large square columns and posts, will create undesirable poison arrow in the garden, while rounded supports will allow the energy to flow harmoniously.

Garden structures

Above: Archways will help slow down the movement of beneficial energy down a long path. The statue at the end of the path can be used to deflect any poison arrows generated if the path were straight.

Opposite: Too many straight lines in both garden structures and furniture will generate too many poison arrows. Place Christmas tree lights along the pergola structural supports and place flowers and shrubs potted in rounded tubs around the front of each column. Cover the table with a floral patterned cloth and keep the rounded shrubs in the center of the table.

It is important that garden structures do not create poison arrows that cause disruptions in the flow of energy in the garden. These arrows are particularly harmful in the front garden – you rely on the garden and entrance being well positioned and set out to attract and receive a flow of beneficial energy from the environment along your street.

Stand by your front door and see if there are any sharp angles created, in particular, by your gateway. If you have a pergola or roofed gate over your driveway or entrance, make sure that the structure is not casting any poison arrows in the direction of your front door or toward any part of your garden.

If the roofline is hitting a particular area, consider adding a decorative or practical feature to the end of the roofline – perhaps a drainpipe leading down to the ground, or a small terracotta figurine (one on each side of the roof for balance), or a pair of bells, pagoda-style.

Grow a tall shrub in front of any vertical timber, stone or brick post that is part of the entrance to your property, and in front of any other sharply angled structures in the garden. If you wish to sit under a pergola that has a number of exposed beams overhead, plant climbers that will grow up to cover them and that will create an auspicious circulation of beneficial energy – try wisteria, clematis, honeysuckle, and scented jasmine.

While you are waiting for these plants to grow, you can counter the overwhelming downward-bearing energy created by the beams of the pergola by tying red ribbons on each beam and hanging a basket of flowers and plants from each of the major structural beams.

Soften the corners of garden sheds and other small buildings in the garden with plants or by hanging a crystal or wind chime in front of the corners. An ideal location for your child's play house is in the northeast, as it is believed that the energy from this direction, which represents the attainment of wisdom and knowledge, is excellent for helping children learn and develop their skills.

Fire pits, barbecues and outdoor ovens are best situated in the south, and should be constructed out of Earth-related materials, such as brick; use only a small amount of Metal in the structure. Metal and Fire create an inharmonious energy, while Fire and Earth are symbolic of a harmonious flow of energy, which will help reduce the number of fire-related accidents.

Garden lighting

Above: Upward-pointing lights should be used to counterbalance any oppressively positioned walls.

Opposite: Lights will help stimulate the energy down a dark corridor, pathway or tunnel.

Below: Diffused lighting allows the beneficial flow of energy through the garden.

Exotic-looking lanterns filled with patterned and colored glass, scattered citronella candles in tall glasses, bamboo flares and Christmas tree lights tucked into dense, dark greenery are magical touches that not only make the garden look great in the evening but also stimulate the circulation of beneficial energy around the garden, creating a soulful, visually pleasing experience.

Garden lighting essentially generates yang energy; it can be used to balance the yin elements in the garden, such as water features, and in dark corners of the garden where the energy may slow down too much. Since lights represent the Fire element, and the elements of Fire and Water clash, it is not recommended that you place lights in water features (for example, in fountains). However, lights shining on water is good Feng Shui. Generally, avoid strong, glaring lights unless you are remedying the flow of disruptive energy created by a poison arrow.

Garden lighting can also improve security in your property. Often security is breached at points where poison arrows hit a fence line, window or door. For instance, keep a light permanently on (use a low wattage light to keep the cost and energy use low) on the back porch if you can see a pole, roofline or the corner of a garden structure directly in line with the back door.

Use an upward-pointing light in your front yard if the street is higher than the ground floor level of your house.

In Feng Shui, it is important to light garden pathways and gateways. This helps the beneficial energy – not to mention your evening guests! – find the way to your front door or through your garden to your outdoor dining setting without mishap. Should any accidents occur outdoors in the evening, rectify the poor energy flow in that area by adding some lighting. The extra light will help everyone see where they are going, and will also add yang energy to stimulate the flow of qi in the area.

Also add light in the southerly part of your garden, particularly in your front yard, which represents the public side of your life, to attract a promotion or acknowledgment at work (page 37). The south sector of the garden relates to fame and acknowledgment – lights placed in this area are particularly effective in enhancing the reputation of the residents.

Above: Small courtyards can be created at the corner of a house or in the middle of a horseshoe-shaped home to make it look regular and to help encourage the flow of energy.

Opposite: A terrace, as well as a courtyard or balcony, can be added to make the outline of a house or an apartment square or rectangular.

Below: You can help energy to flow in a beneficial way in even the smallest gardens. This small garden features curved rocks and a winding path to maximize the movement of energy.

Feng shui in small spaces: intimate designs

Feng shui gardening principles can benefit even the smallest garden, whether it is tucked into a small courtyard (page 72), along a terrace (page 73), on a balcony (page 74) or in a simple window box (page 75). In fact, these small gardens can help encourage the flow of beneficial energy in the house, remedying any architectural design features that have had a negative effect on one or more of the eight aspirations of life (pages 34–35).

In Feng Shui, a square or rectangular house is an auspicious shape for the flow of energy around both the property and the owner's life. A square shape symbolizes the Earth element (page 20); the rectangular shape symbolizes Wood (page 23).

Use the instructions on pages 28–29 to work out which area of your home each of the eight aspirations relates to. If your home is not a regular shape, you may find that the area of your home that corresponds to a particular aspiration is very small or even completely missing. This can lead to a poor energy flow in that particular aspiration.

For example, if the relationships area of your home is missing or smaller in size than the other areas, you may find that you experience problems and difficulties in your marriage. Try using the garden to symbolically extend the missing area of your home and so rectify any problems in the energy flow in that aspiration area.

Sometimes courtyards, decking, balconies and terraces slightly extend the line of the house. In some schools of Feng Shui, these extensions are believed to enhance the generation of energy in the corresponding aspiration. For example, a small deck added to the area relating to fame and acknowledgment attracts this energy to the occupants of the house.

Above: Use very large objects in your small garden only if your space is too shady or is overly yin in energy.

Opposite: No matter how small your garden, always make sure that you feel comfortable in the space.

Below: Place a potted plant or hang a crystal in front of all the corners of the building that are affecting your small garden, as these create poison arrows that may make you feel uncomfortable in this space.

Small-scale gardens: beauty and harmony in miniature

One of the most important Feng Shui issues concerning small-scale gardens is proportion. Garden structures, furniture, plants and ornaments that would suit a large open space must not be used in a small garden, as the yang energy created by these overwhelmingly large features will unbalance the flow of energy; you may find that you avoid sitting in that area or that arguments frequently seem to erupt there.

Although using overly large elements may add a dramatic effect – and they may be conversation pieces – only consider using them if your small-scale garden is generating too much yin energy.

When the garden is strongly yin in energy, try planting a few specimen plants that have a strong character, either in terms of dramatic plant or leaf shapes, or color, or rarity. Consider incorporating plants that resonate with the element of Fire (page 24), particularly in the south of the garden. However, most small-scale gardens should be created so that they provide a fluid balance between yin and yang energies (pages 14–15), and among the five elements (pages 18–25).

Generally, make sure that there is a balance between shady and sunny areas, even in the smallest garden space. The smaller your space, the more choosy you should be about what you need to incorporate into the garden to signify a balance between the elements. Choose well-crafted, small-scale garden ornaments, such as a pretty wall fountain, beautiful mosaics, Christmas tree lights, an attractive metal sculpture or a small hedge of boxwood to symbolize the presence of the five Chinese elements in your garden.

If your small-scale garden is being used to fill in an area missing in one of the aspirations in your home, focus your attention on the corner or wall that is being extended to complete the shape of your house. Do this by hanging a lamp or planting a tree to mark the extended corner, or planting a row of shrubs to extend along the entire wall.

Courtyards

Courtyards offer the opportunity, in Feng Shui terms, of expanding your house space to make it regular in shape, so that beneficial energy flows auspiciously around your property and life. This area also gives you the opportunity to create a private "garden room" that extends your living areas and brings more of the garden's beauty and energy into your life.

Courtyards are often situated at the back of the house. This is a yin energy area, and you can easily make this space a lovely private oasis where you can regain your composure and relax after a stressful day. The right amount of yin energy invites a quieter, more contemplative mood; make sure that this area does not become overgrown, cluttered or too shady.

Observe the cycle of the seasons and the various positions of the sun, and note at what times of the year the courtyard becomes too sunny (or too yang) or too shady (or too yin). On a seasonal basis, incorporate ornaments or Feng Shui cures that symbolize yin or yang energies (pages 14–15) into the courtyard.

If the space is too sunny, add a large umbrella covered with fabric that is either a plain unbleached or off-white colored fabric or that is decorated with stripes or shapes in a yin color such as blue or green. If the energy is too yin, incorporate a yang element, such as Christmas tree lights encircling the entire space.

As courtyards tend to be small, another way of encouraging energy to flow around the space is to use gentle sounds that travel well by bouncing off the courtyard walls and fence. Incorporate wall fountains facing north or east, or metal wind chimes facing west.

Above and left: Rounded pots and healthy, lush growth helps the beneficial flow of energy around even the smallest garden.

Terraces

Terraces are excellent ways of dealing with sloping land. Feng shui practitioners believe that the ideal situation is for land to slope gently from the east to the west so that a property is higher on the east side than on the west. Terraces that face west or sunken gardens on the west side of the garden are considered very auspicious.

The west is believed to correspond to the disruptive energy of the Celestial Tiger, which is best kept subdued and in balance with the rest of the celestial creatures by being placed at a slightly lower level. Where the westerly part of the garden is raised, the flow of unsettling energy is increased; it should be dissipated by screens and other Feng Shui cures (pages 76–93).

If your terrace faces west, do not raise this area visually by planting trees or shrubs that can grow to a great height. Keep the plantings low and harmonious, incorporating rounded shrubs or trees that correspond to a westerly energy, such as Japanese maples. Add objects and plantings that symbolize the Fire element, such as lighting and triangular shrubs or trees, and avoid using objects and plants that correspond to the Earth element.

A stone or brick wall can be used to create a terraced effect in the garden if the terrace is in the northeast or southwest. To visually soften the wall of a terrace, plant a hedge in front of the wall. Do not grow ivy or another creeper on the wall, as the yin energy of the plant will overpower the yang energy of the wall. Consider making a terrace out of wooden railway ties, if your terrace will be in the easterly or southerly areas of your garden. Retain the natural slope of the land but incorporate a waterfall if the area is in the northerly section.

Above and right: Terracing of the landscape should look as natural as possible or incorporate curved lines or rounded water features.

Balconies

Balconies are excellent ways of highlighting attractive views and inviting the energy of nature into an apartment space. However, as a balcony is often accessed by sliding doors, usually made of large panes of glass, it is particularly important in Feng Shui terms for the balcony not only to frame or create a pleasant view but also to contain the energy that may otherwise travel straight from the apartment's main entrance and out through the balcony.

In Feng Shui it is most inauspicious for the back door or the balcony sliding doors to be exactly opposite the front door, because the energy will tend to rush straight through the space without circulating, and thus without giving any benefits to the space. This can easily be remedied by softening the lines of the balcony. Use screens and plants to create a lush garden on the balcony – this will encourage the energy to flow back into the apartment. Use only plants that will thrive with little water, as balconies tend to trap the heat of the day and dry out plants, or be very careful to water frequently during hot weather. To balance the potential yang effects of a balcony garden, particularly in summer, install a water fountain in the north, east or southeast areas – these are supported by the element of Water (page 22) – either on a wall or nestled among the plants.

Below left: Arrange potted plants so that each corner of a rectangular-shaped balcony is covered. Also use pots that are either round or that have rounded corners.

Below right: If your balcony is overly sunny and dry, balance this yang energy by including pots of yin-colored flowers.

Window boxes

Window boxes are a delightful way of screening an unpleasant view and generating a flow of positive energy into your home. Both balconies and window boxes, no matter which area they are in, can enhance the flow of energy through a particular aspiration area (pages 34–45).

It is important that the plants used in the window box are compatible, nurturing each other's growth, and that the window boxes are positioned in windows that are not exposed to strong winds and harsh, sunny conditions.

Attractive flowering plants that could be used for sunny window boxes include white, pink or scarlet nicotianas, blue or purple salvias and miniature roses. Many of these grow upright and will cover the lower half of a window with pretty flowers. For shady window boxes, try ferns, hostas and other moisture-loving plants.

In some Feng Shui schools it is believed that the best type of window for the auspicious circulation of beneficial energy is the kind that opens outward. Outward-opening windows would tend to preclude a window box unless the top of the box were below the windowsill and it contained plants that cascade over the window box in rounded shapes, such as fuchsias, or that spread and spill over the edge of the window box, such as yellow or white zinnias and lobelias.

Below left: Window boxes, when planted with flowers and herbs that grow tall or that spill over the edge, help soften the architectural lines of a Western house, lessening the impact of any poison arrows created by those long, straight lines.

Below right: Window boxes attract positive energy into a home as the windows frame the view outside enhanced by the flowers of a window box. Window boxes can also be used to help screen out undesirable views.

Feng Shui Cures

Solving energy flow problems

Above: Fierce-looking creatures that can be used for protection should always be positioned looking away from your home. You don't want this strong yang energy constantly aimed at a section of your property.

Opposite: Feng Shui cures that move in the breeze gently help beneficial energy to keep flowing in potentially stagnant areas, such as at the end of a pathway or in a dark, overly yin area of the garden.

Feng shui cures are objects that symbolically correct energy flow problems, such as poison arrows (pages 80–81) and stagnation, which manifests in the accumulation of clutter.

There are eight general Feng Shui cures – reflective objects or lights (pages 82–83), colors (pages 84–87), sounds (and flutes and fans) (pages 88–89), electrical (pages 90–91), statues and rocks (page 92) and pets (and mobiles and flags) (page 93). It is believed that each Feng Shui cure is particularly effective in a certain aspiration. Check the table below to see the relationship between Feng Shui cures, aspirations and compass directions:

Compass direction	Aspiration	Feng shui cure
North	Career	Movement/mobiles and flags
South	Fame and acknowledgment	Reflective objects, lights
East	Family and health	Electrical equipment
West	Children and creativity	Rocks and statues
Northwest	Mentors, useful friends in authority, travel	Sounds
Northeast	Knowledge and study	Color
Southwest	Relationships	Flutes and fans
Southeast	Wealth	Plants and pets

Plants can also be used as Feng Shui cures. A massing of plants in the southeast segment of the garden will help correct the flow of energy to your finances. There are even particular plants that are believed to bring good luck in your wealth sector, such as a clumping golden bamboo which, because of its similarity in color to gold, is believed to encourage the flow of wealth to the owner of the garden. Bamboo is also symbolic of strength and longevity; growing this plant at the rear of your property will stimulate a nurturing energy in your life.

Other plants that encourage prosperity include the jade or money tree (*Portulacaria afra*) with its coin-shaped leaves, and the large, green perforated-leaf monstera (*Monstera deliciosa*), which needs to be planted in a sheltered area, preferably in the southeast area of the garden.

If your sewage outlet is in the southeast area of the garden, consider covering the potentially overwhelming yin energy emanating from this outlet with a couple of ivy plants potted in a rounded container. Ivy and various scented plants are believed to be able to absorb negative energy from poison arrows, any emotional instability of the household, and undesirable smells emanating from the sewage outlet, compost heap or a nearby factory.

The following pages show how to place a certain object in a particular position in the garden to improve the feelings of tranquility and harmony in the garden and home.

Opposite, clockwise from top left: The sound of water trickling through bamboo helps activate energy; vibrant yang-colored plantings help balance the overly yin energy of a large pond; bamboo may be used to distribute positive energy and deflect poison arrows; a garden statue helps anchor fast-flowing energy.

Above: There are many specialized Chinese Feng Shui cures that are easily available from Feng Shui practitioners and various new age stores. This cure is made of coins tied together with auspicious red thread. It helps distribute beneficial energy and will attract wealth into the home.

Deflecting poison arrows

Dealing with poison arrows is one of the most important steps in creating a garden or home full of harmony and balance. First, work out whether or not your garden is being hit by poison arrows. Then clear the clutter in the garden; it is possible that the clutter has become a type of "shield" against the negative energy of poison arrows. Never use clutter as a way of rectifying energy flow problems – all it does is stagnate energy further. However, clutter can be an indicator that a poison arrow is present.

The following objects and environmental features create poison arrows, which may be affecting your property:

- a straight road aimed at your property
- a tree with a prominent central trunk
- a telephone or flagpole
- the lines of a building
- a straight driveway or garden bed
- a narrow corridor of property by the side of the house
- a prominent corner of a house (your own or your neighbor's)
- a prominent architectural feature of the house, such as an angled roofline, a column or a balustrade, or something in the garden, such as a pergola.

There are numerous ways of minimizing the effect of poison arrows. Many of the Feng Shui cures, such as water (pages 90–91), mirrors (pages 82–83), plants (pages 54–55), solid objects (page 92) and objects that move,

Above and left: Bright, cheerful plants and garden ornaments, when positioned correctly, can successfully be used to counter and disperse the force of a poison arrow.

such as mobiles and wind chimes (page 93), can be used to deflect or disperse the negative energy of poison arrows.

Crystals are also an effective way of dispersing negative energy. A particularly useful multipurpose crystal that can be used in the garden is a clear quartz crystal, which must be washed thoroughly in running water before being used for any sort of work with energy. For example, place or hang the crystal over a pile of stubborn clutter to help clear the energy in the area, or hang it in a tree or shrub that has recently had to be pruned.

Where should a Feng Shui cure be placed so that it most effectively deflects poison arrows? If a poison arrow is created within your property, place the Feng Shui cure immediately in front of the object or feature causing the poison arrow. In a garden, plants and other garden features, such as evergreen shrubs, climbing plants and landscaped ponds, can also be used to deflect or disperse poison arrows.

If a poison arrow is created by an object that can be moved, consider doing that – Feng Shui cures should be used only for features that are impracticable to move. One of the reasons for restricting the number of cures you use is that too many cures can in themselves upset energy as their shielding energy accumulates.

Stand immediately in front of the offending feature, such as a corner, and see where the poison arrows hit. Poison arrows travel in straight lines, and can radiate in many directions. Place a Feng Shui cure, such as a crystal or wind chime, immediately in front of a corner. If the offending feature is off site (for example, across the road), place the Feng Shui cure between it and an important feature in your home that it is affecting, such as your front door.

Above and right: Corners are notorious culprits for the creation of poison arrows. Shield each corner in a garden with a plant, making sure that it continues to thrive in that position.

Light

Light is an extremely useful and effective Feng Shui cure and can be incorporated in the garden in the form of garden lighting (see pages 66–67), or as objects that reflect light, such as shiny metal balls that can be tucked in among the plants, mirrors that can be hung from the fence, and even water surfaces. This Feng Shui remedy is useful not only for stimulating stagnant areas, particularly in the corners of a garden, but also to combat poison arrows.

The corners of the garden and the house deserve close attention. If your garden is an irregular shape, such as an L shape, identify the protruding corner – it creates a flow of negative energy in the diametrically opposite direction. Try dealing with the corner by planting an evergreen shrub there.

If the corner is created by a fence, place a mirror on either side of the corner of the fence. In Feng Shui, using mirrors like this is believed to create the illusion that the walls do not exist and gives the impression that your garden extends further than it does. This cure can also be used to "disguise" a corner of your house that is protruding into your garden. Mirrors can also be used in a garden purely to give a sense of space; this is especially useful in a courtyard garden.

Be careful with your placement of mirrors, as they are very powerful tools for moving energy about. Placing a mirror directly in front of the entrance to your garden, for instance, is believed to deflect the movement of the energy directly out of the area, which can lead to a sense of stagnation and disharmony in your garden. Instead, place the mirror so that it reflects a beautiful part of your garden or so that it disguises an undesirable feature.

A bagua, with a mirror at its center, can be used to deflect poison arrows aimed at your garden or home by environmental features or objects that are not on your property, such as a straight road, a driveway, a pole or a sharply angled roof. Hang the bagua mirror over the lintel of your front door so that it is pointing at the foot of the attacking object.

Opposite, clockwise from top left: Christmas tree lights are a fabulous way of gently stimulating energy in a stagnant area; white flowers, which are yang in energy, can lift dark areas of the garden; a balance of light and dark areas in the garden helps generate the flow of beneficial energy; yin baguas are used to protect against poison arrows, the mirror helping to deflect negative energies.

Below: Round, reflective objects in the garden help deflect and disperse any poison arrows aimed at the area. Use in spots at the end of a long path or near a corner where the garden edgings meet.

Color

Above: Brightly colored hyacinths can be planted to stimulate yang energy in a spot, such as under a tree, that may be too yin in energy.

Opposite: Orange flowers provide a burst of yang energy, which can be used in the front garden to attract beneficial energy into your property or to balance the yin energy of your back garden.

The color of plants, ornaments, flags, lanterns and panels of mosaics, as well as of walls, doors and furniture in the garden, can help stimulate the flow of energy around the garden to enhance a feeling of harmony and balance.

In dark areas of the garden, which can become overly yin in energy, place an object that is yang in color (white or a bright or light color). White, silver or gold can be used to minimize the effect of overbearing beams in a pergola or arbor, for example. Similarly, in an overly yang space in the garden – a dry, raised garden bed, for instance – position an object or garden structure that is yin in color (black or muted, dark colors such as dark green).

To decide what type of object you should use in an affected area, go back to the bagua template you made (see the instructions on pages 28–29 and 34–35). Work out which direction the area is facing, as this will indicate which element governs the area. Then see pages 18–25 to find out what objects correspond to the relevant direction and element, and to see which color range corresponds to which element. The color you use in the area must be related to an element that is compatible with that of the area. Remember, each element can be stimulated by yang (bright) or calmed by yin (muted) versions of a particular color. If a stagnant area of the garden is in the east, for example, and the area leads to a wooden gate in the fence or to a small tool shed, consider painting the gate or the shed in a yang color, such as yellow or beige.

If a garden bed is affected, then depending on the area the garden bed is in, you can incorporate plantings in the colors of the corresponding element to stimulate a harmonious flow of energy.

Black and white are considered lucky colors in Chinese philosophy. They are used to represent the traditional symbol of yin and yang, the black symbolizing yin and the white representing yang. Red and yellow/gold are the two other "lucky" colors that you can use, particularly in your front yard, to attract luck and success.

What colors should you choose for the plants in your garden? As your front yard corresponds to yang energy, it is important to focus on colors that are eye catching and bright here, so that you attract a flow of

beneficial energy from the environment in front of your home. Use reds, oranges and yellows in the front garden. Plants with these color schemes are usually sun loving, so they require a sunny position.

The back garden corresponds to yin energy. To create a harmonious and balanced feeling in the back garden so you can use it for contemplation and relaxation, use yin colors: soothing blues and purples and dark lush greens or pale-colored flowers, and plants that have silver or gray foliage.

Keep your color scheme simple, and be careful to keep a sense of balance in your use of colors, as too many colors and patterns can become clutter. When you use color as a Feng Shui cure, remember that even a small portion of that color is enough to help stimulate the flow of energy.

Use the following table to help you decide where to plant your favorite flowers for the most auspicious flow of energy in your garden.

Color	Yin or Yang	Front yard or back yard	Auspicious direction	Flower suggestions
Blue	yin	back yard	east, southeast	blue violets blue verbena lobelia
Purple	yin	back yard	north	heartsease hyacinth lavender
Red	yang	front yard	south	red dahlia red geranium red hibiscus
Orange/ yellow	yang	front yard	southwest, northeast	nasturtium wallflower yellow zinnia
White	yang	front yard	west, northwest	honesty snow drop white tulip

Opposite, clockwise from top left: Paper daisies – bright, cheerful flowers that resonate with both yang energy and the element of Earth should be planted near your front gate to attract the flow of lucky energy; Cherry blossom – when this plant flowers, it creates a strong, vibrant yang energy that celebrates the joy of spring; Artemesia – this plant (and others with silvery, green foliage) is yin in energy, but can be used to brighten any shady nook; Magnolia – the scent of the magnolia when it blossoms lifts the spirit and helps stimulate the flow of energy.

Above: Purple is usually a yin color that can be used to tone down an area that feels too yang in energy. However, nature has provided many vibrant purple flowers that can be used as accents of yang energy in the garden that feels too yin – perhaps where an area is too shady or near a large body of water.

Below: Red flowers must be used sparingly in any garden. As these flowers often thrive in sunny areas, avoid mass plantings or balance the red with shrubs, possibly evergreens that can handle some exposure to the sun.

Sound

The sound of wind chimes, bells or bamboo flutes is an attractive way to stimulate the energy in a garden, as long as the sounds are melodious and the wind chimes or flutes are positioned in a sheltered part of the garden. When you are experiencing high winds, make sure the chimes or flutes are removed, so they do not make an inordinate amount of noise, thus creating a flow of disturbing energy.

Before clearing the garden of clutter and overgrowth and implementing some permanent Feng Shui strategies to stimulate the flow of beneficial energy, ring a harmonious-sounding bell in and over all the areas where the energy appears to be stagnant.

Ring or strike the bell sharply, but not vigorously, so you are creating a mellow sound – rather than a din – to clear the stagnant energy that has accumulated. You will know that the energy in a particular area is reactivated when you sense that the colors in the area appear brighter or the soil and the plants smell sharper. You may also sense that the air feels clearer.

The sound of a bell will reactivate the flow of energy, but to further encourage the flow of new energy, hang the bell, or a set of wind chimes or bamboo flutes, in the affected area. You will find the sound they make will imbue the space with a sense of peace and tranquility, reclaiming the area as a place to relax.

Chimes and flutes can also be used to disperse the flow of poison arrows along a straight garden path or from a protruding corner. Place the chimes or flutes in front of the protruding corner or at a place at the end of the path. A particularly long path, such as one that runs the full length of your house, allows the energy to build up speed and become too powerful; it may be an idea to place chimes or flutes at several points.

If you enjoy sitting under a pergola, you will need to do something to disperse the downward energy that the main beams above you will project upon your head. Hang some wind chimes from the beams, or the beam under which you tend to sit, to counteract this energy.

Hang a metal wind chime in a northern or northwestern area of the garden; bamboo flutes are best positioned in the southern, southeastern or eastern area of your garden.

Above: The gentle trickling of water from a fountain head soothes the flow of strong yang energy in a sunny part of a garden and can balance the energy of those dry, dusty areas.

Opposite: Natural-looking water features are an extremely beneficial part of a garden designed according to Feng Shui principles. However, make sure that the water flows gently. The constant sound of strong rushing water can be overstimulating and can delete the energy around it.

Feng Shui garden tip

Nature's own sounds are best appreciated in the garden, so provide a protective environment for birds.

Above: Although fountains can disperse poison arrows, it is still beneficial to cover any surrounding corners with a rounded garden ornament.

Opposite: Water features and their surroundings should be as rounded or curved as possible, in imitation of Nature.

Below: Water features help not only to nourish the soul, but also to refresh the flow of beneficial energy in the garden.

Water

A water feature is another way to introduce the Feng Shui remedy of sound, especially if the water feature is constructed so that water falls from a height (see also pages 88–89). The sound of falling water is relaxing and is an excellent, gentle way to stimulate qi in a garden.

The words "Feng Shui" actually refer to the movement of the wind and water, giving us a clue as to how qi should ideally flow. Like wind and water, qi flows around the objects in its environment, but over time it also has the ability to affect and mold these objects.

Although water is a gentle cure, it is also an extremely powerful one. In an area that has too much yang energy, install a small waterfall or other water feature that allows water to fall and be recycled; such a water feature would benefit an area in the garden where the garden beds are drying out or an area where a straight path ends.

Install a circular water feature in an area where the paths and subdivisions of the garden create a rectangular pattern full of straight lines. The nurturing energy of this Feng Shui cure will nourish these areas and bring yin energy into the garden to help evoke a soothing, calming atmosphere. Water features are excellent ways of "curing" or dissipating negative energy, which can be created in a number of ways – by a poison arrow, an unpleasant view in the immediate vicinity, or the unchecked flow of the usually disruptive energy from the west.

If the water feature includes a pump to help the water flow and be recycled, then the Feng Shui cure is being combined with two other cures – movement (page 93) and mechanical/electric. Mechanical cures include your child's swings or other moving play area equipment and such common garden ornaments as sundials.

A water feature can be used to maximum benefit in a number of different aspirations: the area that corresponds to wealth (southeast), the area that corresponds to the family and health aspiration (east), and the area that corresponds to the career aspiration (north).

When designing a pond for your garden, choose shapes that curve slightly as if to encompass a portion of your house. For example, use a kidney-shaped pond and position it so that the two ends of the shape are pointing towards the house.

Solid objects

Solid objects are an excellent cure for anchoring energy. They are also effective in balancing the flow of disruptive energy from the west. Solid objects can range from heavy artistic sculptures and statues (pages 58–59) to a natural formation of heavy rocks. These objects, which must be rounded and without jagged edges, are great for stabilizing unsettled energy in areas where arguments tend to flare up.

It is important that the objects are not only solid but also heavy, as this Feng Shui cure is designed to stabilize any overly yang energy. This is a yin energy cure, and should not be used in areas where the energy appears too stagnant, such as deep corners. If you have such an object – a sculpture that has been cemented in, for instance – tucked in a dark garden corner, and you cannot easily move it, consider painting it a yang color or lighting it using a bright light.

When choosing a solid object for a feng shui cure, make sure that it does not overwhelm the garden or the house. Also, take care not to place heavy, solid objects in the path of your front door, as this will interfere with the flow of positive energy into the house.

This cure can stabilize unsettled energies, so if you are suffering from any problems at work, such as keeping staff or being fired, install a heavy sculpture, pedestal or urn in the area of the garden that corresponds with your career aspiration (pages 34–35 and pages 42–43).

Above left: Empty pots that are rounded are excellent ways of anchoring fast-flowing energy, encouraging it to slow down and move around the curves of the pot.

Left: A massing of rocks can be used successfully in a large garden. Never use objects that are out of proportion to the rest of your garden space.

Movement

Movement can be introduced as a cure in a garden in a number of ways and can be used in areas that correspond to several aspirations. For instance, this cure can be effectively used to stimulate energy in the wealth aspiration (southeast) by keeping pets in the area.

In the southeastern part of your garden, place fish in a pond, or construct an area where your pet would like to be – such as a small aviary, a kennel for your dog, a patch of catnip for your cat or a large, roomy cage for your rabbit – to generate good luck in your finances. Make sure that your pets are healthy and happy – an ill-used animal will attract bad luck to you.

Movement from mobiles and flags can be very effective in stimulating energy in the career aspiration (north) area of your garden. If you are feeling unsure of your career path, focus on this area (see also pages 42–43): install a glass mobile in a sheltered position where it will move gently with a breeze. If you notice that the mobile is constantly becoming tangled, remove it and use another form of movement cure – plant a tree or shrub that encourages butterflies or birds into the garden, for instance.

To attract birds, plant such trees as acacias, birches, crab apples, figs, firs, oaks, pines and spruces. Also consider planting shrubs and flowers such as fuchsias, grevilleas, honeysuckles, and geraniums. To attract butterflies, plant daffodils, lavender, rhododendrons or rosemary.

Above right: Goldfish will help keep the energy of your water feature from becoming stagnant. The flash of red and gold as the fish swim around is also an excellent balance to the yin energy of the pool.

Right: Movement can be seen when the wind ruffles a row of lavender, allowing the scent to waft across the garden.

Above: In summer, vibrant colored flowers celebrate the maturation of yang energy during this time of year.

Below: The rounded, cup shape of the magnolia blossom, as well as its beautiful scent, attracts good qi into the garden in spring.

Tapping into seasonal energy for a lush, healthy garden

Qi is attracted into the garden in many ways (pages 46–67) and prefers to be gently guided through a space in curves and undulating lines and welcomed with melodious sounds, harmonious colors and shapes, tidiness and a sense of balance between yin and yang energies and among the elements. It ebbs and flows according to the environment around it, and is imbued with the energies of yin and yang, as well as of the elements. However, it also ebbs and flows according to the seasons.

When you work in your garden, you will naturally tap into the cyclic nature of seasonal qi as it helps you organize your tasks in the garden. You will find that many of the Feng Shui techniques that have been discussed in this book can be best implemented during particular seasons – this helps you stagger your workload and enjoy the benefits.

In Chinese medicine and philosophies, the way to harmonize the energies of the body and the mind is by tapping into this natural progression and flow of seasonal energy. By doing tasks in your garden during the appropriate season, you will be able to tap into the wisdom that ancient Chinese philosophers have gained over many centuries.

Qi takes on a different energy during each season. There are five seasons in the Chinese calendar – autumn, winter, spring, summer and high summer. High summer, which occurs between July 31 and September 21–23 in the northern hemisphere and between January 31 and March 21–23 in the southern, is the shortest season. Although short, it is one of the most important, as it is the time when yin and yang energies are in perfect balance, bringing forth the first harvest of the annual cycle.

In Chinese philosophies, it is believed that the other four seasons can be categorized as either yin or yang in energy and that the five seasons

correspond to the five elements of Earth, Metal, Wood, Fire and Water (page 96). However, some Feng Shui practitioners acknowledge only four seasons, which are symbolized by the elements of Metal, Wood, Fire and Water. They believe that the Earth element does not have its own season – it simply corresponds to the transitional time between the seasons.

By tapping into these seasonal energies, you will be able to slowly and steadily use the Feng Shui techniques and ideas discussed in this book at appropriate times.

There are some Feng Shui tasks that can be implemented immediately to help the flow of energy around your property. However, to create a garden whose energy will bring luck and success into your life, health and lush growth to your plants, and peace and harmony to your soul, give yourself a bit more time to work with the flow of qi around you.

Above: Splashes of rich reds and yellows relate to the energy of the element of Fire and are useful in stimulating the qi of the garden.

Above: Bright, cheerful hanging containers full of flowers can stimulate the flow of beneficial energy during the summer months.

Below: Beautifully scented roses and a calm, shady spot in the garden can be enjoyed especially in spring and summer. Scented flowers are an excellent way of attracting good qi to a garden.

The seasons and the five elements

The seasons of the Chinese calendar all have their own distinctive energy. Autumn is harvest time, when we dig into the ground to bring forth its fruits. It is the start of a predominance of yin energy, which was previously in balance with the yang energy of high summer. During autumn, the energy of the earth is being gathered in and stored to survive the winter months. Colors such as silver, gold and white, and the corresponding element of Metal (page 21) symbolize this expenditure of energy during harvest time.

Winter is a time of yin energy: energy is being conserved, much as water is stored in a metal bowl. Blacks, browns and other dark and muted yin colors, such as dark blues and purples, represent this time of the year, as well as the nurturing element of Water (page 22).

At spring a major shift in energies occurs, as yang energy begins to rise, though unsteadily. Light greens and blues symbolize spring energies, as does the element of Wood (page 23).

Yang energies are dominant in the season of summer, where the unsteady growth of spring matures and strengthens. Strong bright reds correspond to this season, as does the element of Fire (page 24). The yang energies of summer manifest in the first harvest of the year, during the Chinese season of high summer. This balance of yin and yang corresponds to the energies of the element of Earth (page 20) and the colors yellow and beige.

Feng Shui garden tip

Season	Lucky direction	Unlucky direction
Winter	North	Southeast
Spring	East	West
Summer	South	Northeast
High Summer	Southwest	Northwest
Autumn	West	East

Winter

Winter's energy is predominantly yin in nature. This is the best time to start selecting the Feng Shui strategies you want to use to improve your garden and your life. Use this season to become fully aware of the various Feng Shui principles – winter is the time for study and contemplation.

Use the instructions on pages 28–29 to draw a map of your property. See where your house sits in relation to your garden, whether you have one garden or several gardens to consider, and how the eight aspirations – wealth, fame, relationships, creativity, friends, career, knowledge and health – correspond to areas in your property (pages 34–45).

Identify any aspiration areas that are missing or in need of cleaning. However, do not do any cleaning yet, apart from plant maintenance such as clearing the leaves of your perennials. This is a yin time, when the energy is slow and sluggish – wait until spring, and use its rising energy to make a fresh start in the garden.

Get compass readings and see which direction your garden or gardens face. Determine where north, south, east and west are in relation to your garden and figure out what energies are filtering into your property from these directions. Again, identify places where you will need to do something to rebalance these energies.

Use the introspective energy of winter to map out a "master plan" for your garden for the whole seasonal year. To ensure that the jobs get done, be realistic when making your plan. Concentrate on using spring and fall as the time when you focus on introducing new plants into the garden, while summer and winter can be your time for maintenance.

Above: Use lighting to balance the yin energy of winter. The yang energy of light shining from the house will help encourage the flow of beneficial energy during the most frozen months.

Below: As the energy of the earth has gone underground, spend more of your time indoors, plotting and planning your new Feng Shui designed garden!

Feng Shui garden tip

It is important to go with the flow of the seasonal energies. Never force yourself to do something in the garden if you really don't feel up to it. Similarly, do not make the garden or home a place where the beneficial energy is forced or strictly funneled in curves. Such energy likes to be enjoyed, to meander, and to be guided rather than forced or regimented.

Spring

Spring's energy is new, fresh, and full of yang energy. However, this yang energy has ups and downs – it is strong one day and weak the next. In spring, it is quite usual for one day to be sunny and full of yang energy and the next day to be rainy and miserable, evoking yin energy.

Although spring energy is unstable, it is sympathetic to stimulating new growth, making this an excellent time to plant new trees, shrubs and flowers in your garden. While gardens should have all-year-round interest, spring can be a time of joyous planting

Follow the plans you made in winter (page 97) about what plants you should introduce in your garden to achieve a balance in yin and yang and to harmonize the garden with the energies of the elements (pages 18–25). As the weather warms in spring, perennials will start to reappear in your garden. This is the time to ensure these plants are positioned according to feng shui principles and that the flow of energy around them is balanced.

Spring is also a good time to clear stagnant energy. Do a spring cleaning and unclutter your garden. Also use this time to do something about the poison arrows created by features and objects in your immediate environment.

Plant shrubs or other appropriate plants to screen the negative energy, or use other cures to disperse the poison arrows. Remember to incorporate only one cure at a time, so that the combination of cures itself does not become clutter and so that you can sense whether or not the cure has actually changed the flow of energy in the garden.

Above: The garden experiences a sense of renewal and new growth in spring. This is a good time to clear stagnant energy.

Left: Keep the garden free from clutter and remove dead branches and other garden debris to allow the new energy to spread.

Summer

Summer's energy is maturing and strong, full of yang and the element of Fire. This is a time for entertaining, as well as for building and adding objects to the garden to improve the flow of energy or to consolidate the movement of energy already established.

This is also a good time to concentrate on garden maintenance – make sure all the lights are working, mend the pathways, paint pergolas or other structures, and repair garden stakes and walls made of stone. If your garden beds and paths are rectangular shapes or follow straight lines, this is the time to restructure these areas so that you have only curved paths and garden beds.

Build structures that will help you keep things tidy – construct a shed big enough to house all the tools you need in the garden. Consider adding a structure that works as a greenhouse or one that gives you a space to store the bulbs and seeds you may want to plant in the autumn.

Add yin energy to the garden if the sun is particularly strong and its yang energy is drying out the garden. Water the garden well and consider building a pond or pool to counterbalance the occasional excess of yang energy that can occur in this season.

Shady areas will increase the yin energy in the garden just as excessive light may cause too much yang energy in certain areas. If there is too much glare and light in the garden in summer, use a sunshade or umbrella to create cooler areas. Create a more permanent solution by planting trees or a shaded fern area or by building a vine-covered pergola.

Above right: Red, orange and yellow flowers flourish during the summer months, imbuing the garden with a mature, bright and cheery energy.

Right: Be sure to keep your garden well watered during summer to minimize the effect of the strong yang energy of the sun.

High summer

High summer's energy is a perfect balance between yang (working in the garden) and yin (thinking about ways to improve your garden and life).

This is the time to enjoy the harmonies you have created between yin and yang and the elements, the time when you should start reaping the rewards of all your efforts. Feelings of peace and harmony should be predominant during this time, allowing you to relax and take pleasure in your garden. Use this season to explore new meditative practices, or simply to sit in the garden and enjoy the energy flow.

Take as many breaks as possible in the garden during this season and reap the benefits of your winter plans having come to fruition. The balance between yin and yang means that this is an excellent season to show your garden to others and to entertain friends, family and authority figures. Sharing a garden that is in such harmony will provide many rewards, particularly if you are working toward a balanced family life or are hoping for a promotion.

As this is a time of balance between the energies, allow yin energy to help you think of ways to improve your energy "harvest" next year. Contemplate what you would like to see happen in the next high summer period and look back at what wasn't done in the last cycle of seasons. Keep a journal to track your progress and thoughts – use this as your starting point during the winter months, when you will plan for the next harvest.

Above left: Enjoying the shady part of the garden is an excellent way of escaping the heat of high summer.

Left: Being near yin garden features, such as fountains and swimming pools, balances the yang heat.

Autumn

Autumn's energy is an unstable form of yin energy, where the final vestiges of the earth's yang energy – in the form of fruit and vegetables – are being harvested. This is the time where you find that you are also reaping rewards in your life, as the improved energy flow in the garden will bring a better sense of harmony in the eight aspirations areas (pages 34–45).

This is the season when you need to start conserving your energy and preparing for the winter months. Look at the harvest produced by your garden and see what you can use now and what can be stored for later, possibly in the form of preserves, jams, relishes and other foods that have a long shelf life. In your life, look at what progress you have made and what opportunities have come your way during this season – act on those opportunities now.

In the garden, gather in the harvest and carry out the various tasks that are necessary to maintain your plants. Toward the end of the season, take measures to protect your plants from frost and snow. Clear the garden of any clutter that has accumulated during this unstable but fruitful time, and check that there are no new poison arrows or disruptions in the energy flow.

As you move into a more contemplative period of the seasonal cycle, remember to feel gratitude to the earth and the energy that it has used on your behalf. Consider having a final feast in the garden and sharing some of its produce – use the fruit or vegetables in your cooking, or just decorate the table with flowers and foliage.

Above and right: The autumn garden often needs a great deal of attention during this season as you rake the leaves and entertain your friends, enjoying the garden before the onslaught of winter.

Plant list

Plant name (Common and botanical)	Element	Soil conditions	Favorable aspect
Abelia (*Abelia x grandiflora*)	Earth	Well-drained, enriched soil	Full sun or some shade
Acacia (Wattle) (*Acacia* species)	Earth	Tolerates average soil	Full sun
Apple (*Malus* species)	(A different element according to the season – see pages 18–25)	Well-drained, enriched soil	Full or half sun
Artemisia (see Wormwood)			
Asparagus (*Asparagus officinalis*)	Fire	Well-drained, enriched soil	Full sun
Bamboo (over 120 varieties, including Shibataea *lancifolia*)	Wood	Tolerates most soil conditions, except poorly drained soils	Full sun to partial shade
Basil (*Ocimum basilicum*)	Wood	Rich, moist soil	Full sun or partial shade
Birch (Silver) (*Betula pendula*)	Water	Well-drained soil	Full or half sun
Bird of Paradise (*Strelitzia* species)	Fire	Tolerates average soil	Full sun
Boxwood (English) (*Buxus* species)	Wood/Earth	Tolerates average soil	Full sun
Bromeliad (*Bromeliaceae* species)	Fire	Rich, moist soil	Full sun
California poppy (*Eschscholzia californica*)	Fire	Well-drained, average soil	Full sun
Camellia (*Camellia* species)	Wood	Well-drained, slightly acidic soil	Full or half sun
Catmint (*Nepeta x faassenii*)	Metal	Well-drained soil, likes some lime	Full sun, partial shade
Carpet roses (*Rosa* hybrids)	(Depending on the color – see pages 18–25)	Well-drained, enriched soil	Full sun
Cherry (*Prunus* species) (White, such as "Shirotae")	Metal	Well-drained and compost-enriched soil	Sun with protection from wind
Chili	Fire	Well-drained, enriched soil	Full sun
Chive (*Allium schoenoprasum*)	Water	Well-drained, enriched soil	Full sun

Plant name	Element	Soil conditions	Favorable aspect
Chrysanthemum (*Chrysanthemum* species) (Yellow or orange) (White)	(Depending on the color – see pages 18–25) Earth Metal	Well-drained, enriched soil	Full sun
Clematis (*Clematis* species)	(Depending on the color and the season – see pages 18–25)	Well-drained, enriched soil, tolerates clay soils	Full or half sun
Coprosma ("Looking Glass Plant", variegated leaves) (*Coprosma* "Variegata")	Metal	Moist, rich soil	Full sun or partial shade
Crab apple (*Malus* species)	Metal	Well-drained, rich soil	Full sun
Cyclamen (*Cyclamen* species)	Water	Well-drained, rich soil	Partial shade
Cypress (*Cupressus* species)	Fire	Well drained, average soil	Full sun
Daffodil (*Narcissus* species)	Fire	Well-drained, enriched soil	Full sun or partial shade
Dahlia (*Dahlia* species)	Fire	Well-drained, rich soil	Full sun
Dill (*Anethum graveolens*)	Fire	Moist, enriched soil	Full sun
Dogwood (*Cornus* species)	Water	Well-drained, enriched soil	Full sun with wind protection
Evening primrose (*Oenothera biennis*)	Earth	Tolerates well-drained, average soil	Full sun
Fig (*Ficus carica*)	Wood	Tolerates well-drained, average soil	Full or half sun
Fir (*Abies* species)	Fire	Tolerates well-drained, average soil	Full or half sun
Fuchsia (*Fuchsia* species)	Metal	Well-drained, enriched soil	Sun or partial shade
Gardenia (*Gardenia augusta*)	Metal	Well-drained, enriched soil	Full sun or partial shade
Garlic (*Allium sativum*)	Fire	Fertile, slightly alkaline soil	Full sun
Geranium (scented) (*Pelargonium* species)	(Depending on the color of the flower – see pages 18–25)	Tolerates well-drained, average soil	Full sun
Gladiolus (*Gladiolus* species)	Fire	Fertile, alkaline soil	Full sun
Grevillea (*Grevillea* species)	Metal	Tolerates well-drained, clay-like soils	Full sun or partial shade
Heartsease (*Viola tricolor*)	Water	Well-drained, rich soil	Partial shade

Plant name	Element	Soil conditions	Favorable aspect
Heliotrope (*Heliotropium arborescens*)	Water	Well-drained, rich soil	Full sun or partial shade
Hellebore (*Helleborus* species)	Wood	Moist, alkaline soil	Partial to full shade
Hibiscus (*Hibiscus rosa-sinensis* cultivars)	(Depending on the color of the flower – see pages 18–25)	Well-drained, enriched soil	Full or half sun
Honesty (*Lunaria annua*)	Metal	Tolerates average soil	Partial or full shade
Honeysuckle (*Lonicera* species)	Water	Well-drained, average soil	Partial shade
Hosta (Plaintain Lily) (*Hosta* species)	Wood	Moist, well-drained soil	Partial or full shade
Hyacinth (*Hyacinthus orientalis*)	(Depending on the color – see pages 18–25)	Well-drained, alkaline soil treated with blood and bone before planting	Full sun
Hydrangea (*Hydrangea* species)	Wood/Metal	Moist, enriched soil	Partial or full shade
Iris (*Iris* species)	Fire	Tolerates well-drained, average soil	Full sun
Jade or Money Tree (*Portulacaria afra*)	Wood/Water	Well-drained, enriched soil	Full or half sun
Japanese maple (*Acer* species)	Metal	Well-drained, enriched soil	Full sun
Juniper (*Juniperus* species)	Water	Well-drained, enriched soil	Full sun
Lamb's Ear (*Stachys* species)	Metal	Tolerates well-drained, average soil	Full sun or partial shade
Lavender (*Lavendula* species)	Water/Metal	Tolerates well-drained, average soil	Full sun
Leek (*Allium* species)	Fire	Well-drained soil treated with nitrogen or liquid fertilizer	Full sun or partial shade
Lobelia (*Lobelia* species)	(Depending on the color of the flower – see pages 18–25)	Well-drained, enriched soil	Full sun or partial shade
Lupin (*Lupinus* species)	Fire	Tolerates well-drained, average soil	Full sun
Magnolia (*Magnolia* species)	Water	Well-drained, slightly acidic soil	Full sun or light shade
Marigolds (*Targetes* species)	Earth	Tolerates average soil	Full sun
Mint (*Mentha* species)	Water	Moist, rich soil	Partial shade
Monstera (*Monstera deliciosa*)	Water/Wood	Moist, rich soil	Full or partial shade

Plant name	Element	Soil conditions	Favorable aspect
Nasturtium (*Trapaeolum majus*)	Earth	Tolerates well-drained, average soil	Full sun
Nicotiana (*Nicotiana* species) (White, pink or scarlet)	(Depending on the color – see pages 18–25)	Well-drained, enriched soil	Full sun
Oak (*Quercus* species)	Metal	Well-drained, enriched soil	Full sun
Orange jessamine (*Murraya paniculata*)	Metal	Well-drained, enriched soil	Full sun
Pine (*Pinus* species)	Fire	Tolerates poor soil	Full sun
Pittosporum (*Pittosporum* species)	Wood	Well-drained, enriched soil	Full sun or partial shade
Plum tree (crimson-leafed) (*Prunus* species – including a flowering plum tree *P. cerasifera* "Nigra")	Fire	Fertile soil	Full sun or partial shade
Primrose (*Primula* species)	Earth/Wood	Well-drained, enriched soil	Partial shade
Rhododendron (*Rhododendron* species)	Water	Well-drained, enriched lime-free soil	Partial to full shade
Rockrose (*Cistus* species) (Yellow variety)	Earth	Well-drained soil	Full sun
Rosemary (*Rosmarinus officinalis*) (Prostrate rosemary – *R. officinalis* "Prostratus")	Earth	Well-drained, alkaline soil Tolerates poor soil	Full sun
Roses (*Rosa* species) (Ochre or yellow) (White) (Red)	(Depending on the color – see pages 18–25) Earth Metal Fire	Rich, well-drained soil (add some lime if soil is too acidic)	Full sun
Sage (*Salvia* species) (Garden sage – *S. officinalis*,or golden sage – *S. officinalis* "Variegata") (Blue or purple sage – *S. x superba*)	Water	Rich, well-drained soil (add some lime if soil is too acidic)	Full sun
Snapdragon (*Antirrhinum majus*)	Fire	Rich, well-drained soil	Full sun for part of the day and partial shade
Spruce (*Picea* species)	Fire	Well-drained but tolerates poor soil	Full sun

Plant name	Element	Soil conditions	Favorable aspect
Tea tree (*Leptospermum* species)	Water	Well-drained soil	Full sun
Thyme (*Thymus* species)	Water	Average soil with some lime	Full sun, partial shade
Tomato (Red) (*Lycopersicum esculentum*)	Fire	Well-drained, enriched soil	Full sun
Tulip (*Tulipa* species)	Fire	Fertile soil with some lime to counterbalance an acid soil	Full or half sun
Verbena (*Verbena* species) (Red and pink) (Blue and purple) (White)	Fire Water Metal	Well-drained, enriched soil	Full sun with some partial shade
Violet (*Viola* species) (Black, purple and blue)	Water	Rich, well-drained soil	Partial shade
Wallflower (*Cheiranthus cheiri*)	Earth	Well-drained soil with some lime	Full sun for part of the day
Wisteria (*Wisteria* species)	Water	Tolerates well-drained, average soil	Full or half sun
Wormwood (*Artemisia* species)	Metal	Tolerates well-drained, average soil	Full sun
Yarrow (*Achillea millefolium*)	Metal	Tolerates well-drained, average soil	Full sun
Yew (*Taxus* species)	Earth	Well-drained, enriched soil	Full sun
Zinnia (*Zinnia* species) (Yellow) (White)	Earth Metal	Rich, well-drained soil	Full sun

Glossary

bagua (also known as pa kua)	an octagonal shape representing the eight aspirations of life, corresponding compass directions, and other information relevant for the practice of the art of Feng Shui
chi	see *qi*
dragon	The Green Dragon is a Celestial creature symbolizing the wise and cultured energy of the east.
eight aspirations	The eight aspirations in Feng Shui are wealth and prosperity, fame and acknowledgment, relationships, creativity and children, mentors and travel, career, knowledge, and family and health.
elements	In Feng Shui, five elements are recognized: Earth, Wood, Water, Metal and Fire.
Feng Shui	the Chinese art of placement and design to enhance the flow of universal energy
phoenix	The Red Phoenix is a Celestial creature symbolizing the lucky energy of the south.
poison arrow	a harmful shaft of energy created by long straight corridors, paths or roads, or by sharp angles created by rooflines, corners, etc.
qi (also known as *chi*)	the Chinese name for universal energy
sha qi	see *poison arrow*
tiger	The White Tiger is a Celestial creature symbolizing the unsettled energy of the west.
trigram	There are eight trigrams, which are made up of a combination of three broken and/or unbroken lines and which correspond to the eight aspirations.
tortoise	The Black Tortoise is a Celestial creature symbolizing the nurturing energy of the north.
yang	male or active energy
yin	female or passive energy

Acknowledgments

The photographer would like to thank the following for their kindness in allowing their gardens to be photographed.

Designers

Michael Cooke, Australia: 45 bottom, 81 bottom

Faulkner & Chapman, Australia: 61

Peter Fudge, Australia: 8, 25, 43 top left,
   46 bottom, 63 center, 69, 73 bottom, 78 bottom
   left, 100 bottom

Imperial Gardens, Australia: cover, back cover 1st left,
   11, 32 left, 35, 36, 37, 40 bottom, 43 bottom left,
   44 top, 48, 68, 78 top left, 89, 90 bottom, 91,
   92 bottom, 93 top, 99 bottom, 102

Marc Peter Keene, Japan: 63 left, 67, 71

Webb Landscapes, Australia: 65

Amanda Oliver, Australia: 21 top

Locations/Garden owners

Judy Andrews, Australia: 60

Butchart gardens, Canada: 12

Chenies Manor, UK: 25 bottom

Chinese Gardens, Singapore: 13

Corinda, Australia: 49 center

Cowra Japanese Garden, Australia: 5

Villa Ephrussi de Rothschild, France: back cover far
   right, 32 bottom, 51, 80 bottom

Filoli, USA: 49 left, 98 bottom

Henderson Garden, Australia: 26, 72 bottom

Meadowbrook Farm, USA: 21 bottom, 54, 90 top

Mistilis garden, Australia: 63 right

Valerie Murray, Canada: 9

Nooroo, Australia: back cover 2nd right, 15,
   24 bottom, 101

Polly Park, Australia: 22, 78 top right

Joan Paterson, Canada: 17, 33 center, 41 top, 74

Pondokkie, Australia: 52

Pukekura Park, Australia: 57, 73 top

Red Cow Farm, Australia: 50, 64, 81 top, 96 bottom

Redlands, Australia: 46 top, 47

Singapore Botanical Gardens: 19, 43 bottom right

Anne Spencer, Australia: back cover 2nd left, 40 top

Turn End, UK: 92 top

Le Vasterival, France: 94 top, 95

West Green, UK: 33 left

White Barn Inn, USA: 97 top

All photographs by Leigh Clapp, except for the following by Brett Boardman: 70 top, 79, 83 bottom left

Index

aspirations, 26–27, 34–45, 68, 70, 76, 90, 93, 97, 108
career, 34, 42, 90, 92, 93
creativity and children, 34
fame, acknowledgement, promotion, 34, 37, 66, 68
family and health, 34 45, 80
improving prosperity, 34, 36, 79, 90, 93
knowledge and study, 34, 44
mentors and travel, 34, 41
relationships, 34, 38, 68

bagua, 26–9, 34, 82, 84, 108
balcony, 68, 74
bamboo, 24, 36, 45, 55, 79, 103
barbecue, 18, 19, 24, 25, 37, 64
birds, attracting, 93
butterflies, attracting, 93

celestial animals, 10, 73
  black tortoise, 12, 42, 58, 108
  green dragon, 12, 13, 58, 108
  red phoenix, 12, 16, 58, 108
  white tiger, 12, 13, 58, 108
chi see qi
colour, 84–7
compass directions, 12–13, 16, 26, 29–30, 34, 51–3, 56, 62, 73, 76, 84, 88, 90, 97
  seasons, 96
courtyards, 68, 72
crystals, 44, 64, 70, 81

dead trees, 36, 38
direction see compass directions
dragon, 45, 58, 108
dragon turtle, 58

earth, element see elements
elements, 10, 18–25, 46, 52, 60, 70, 84
  Chinese system of, 18
  destructive cycle, 18
  earth, 10, 18–19, 20, 22, 24 –25, 30, 40, 42, 44, 51, 52, 62, 64, 68, 73, 87, 96
  fire, 10, 18–19, 23–25, 30, 33, 36, 37, 44, 51, 52, 60, 64, 70, 73, 96
  metal, 10, 18–19, 20–25, 30, 36, 40, 42, 51, 52, 60, 62, 64
  plants, 103–107
  productive cycle, 18
  seasons, 94–102
  use of, to reharmonise, 25
  water, 10, 18–23, 25, 30, 36, 40, 42, 51, 52, 74, 96
  wood, 10, 18–25, 30, 37, 45, 51, 52, 62, 68, 96
energy, beneficial, 8, 10
entrance, 46, 48–49

Christmas tree lights, 72, 82
fame see aspirations
Feng Shui, 108
  benefit, 8
  concepts, 10
  cures, 10, 76–93
  elements, use of, 18
  landscape school of, 10
fire see elements
flowers
  artemisia, 21, 87, 103, 107
  camellia, 23, 54, 103

chrysanthemum, 20, 21, 104
cyclamen, 22, 104
daffodil, 24, 93, 104
dahlia, 24, 37, 104
gladioli, 24, 105
grevillea, 93, 105
heliotrope, 49, 105
hosta, 23, 75, 105
hydrangea, 23, 53, 105
iris, 24, 53, 105
marigold, 20, 106
rose, 20, 21, 23, 24, 48, 49, 75, 103, 106
violet, 22, 107
fountains, 56
frog, 58, 60
furniture, 62–3

garden, back, 16, 26, 29, 87
garden, front, 16, 26, 29, 56, 64, 66, 84
goldfish see koi
hammock, 63
hedges, 54–5
herbs
  basil, 23, 103
  catnip, 21, 103
  chive, 22, 53, 104
  dill, 24, 104
  garlic, 24, 104

lavender, 48, 49, 51, 93, 105

mint, 22, 106

parsley, 23

rosemary, 20, 49, 51, 93, 106

sage, 20, 107

thyme, 22, 49, 51, 107

wormwood, 21, 107

yarrow, 21, 107

house placement, 12, 13, 58

koi, 36

light, 82

lighting, garden, 15, 16, 33, 37, 66, 72, 82

longevity, 24, 45

metal see elements

mirrors, 82

movement, 42, 93

ornaments, 60, 72

paths, 13, 16, 46, 48, 49, 50–1, 66

paving, 19, 20, 25, 48, 50–1

pergola, 23, 45, 63, 64

pets, 93

plant shapes, 52–3

poison arrows, 13, 26–27, 32–3, 37–38, 40, 45, 54, 56, 64, 70, 76, 79–82, 88, 98, 108

pond, 22, 36

proportion, 48–9, 70

prosperity, improving see aspirations

pruning, 42, 54, 81

qi, 8, 10, 13, 26, 108

attracting, 46–67

mouth of, 16

relationships see aspirations

rock garden, 20, 40

roofline, 64

screens, 54–5

sculpture, 16, 21, 27, 40, 42, 44, 92

seasons, 94–102

autumn, 94–6, 101

high summer, 94–6, 100

spring, 94–6

summer, 94–6, 99

winter, 94–7

sha qi, 49

see also poison arrows

sheds, 20, 64, 99

site

energy flow, 28–9

surroundings of, 32–3

symmetry and shape, 30

solid objects, 92

sound, 88, 90

statues, 38, 40–42, 58, 92

structures, 64

swimming pool, 22, 56, 58

terrace, 68, 73

trees, 54–5

cherry, 38, 87, 103

conifer, 23, 53

dogwood, 22, 53, 104

English boxwood, 23, 37, 53, 103

magnolia, 22, 87, 106

pine, 24, 93, 106

pittosperum, 23, 106

plum, 24, 106

silver birch, 22, 93, 103

tea tree, 22

yew, 20, 53, 107

water, element see elements

water, in the garden, 13, 22, 88

feature, 15, 18, 22, 27, 30, 33, 36, 42, 56, 58, 88

wind chimes, 33, 72, 81, 88

window, 75

window box, 68, 75

wood, element see elements

yin and yang, 8, 10, 14–15, 30, 33, 42, 54–5, 56, 60, 66, 70, 72, 74, 84, 92, 108

seasonal, 94–102